Praise for the writing of Mechele Armstrong

Dinah's Dark Desire

"Ms. Armstrong writes enchanting characters that are alive and wanton. Pleasing to read and engrossing throughout, I highly recommend this book, especially to anyone who enjoys a ménage."

– P J, *The Erotic Bookworm*

"Ms. Armstrong has given us more than just a ménage story, although the sex is very, very hot; she has given us a satisfying and fulfilling story about three people who are good friends and how they came together as lovers."

– Jo, *Joyfully Reviewed*

Dinah's Christmas Desire

"Dinah, Taylor and Ian are back with a little Christmas delight…Mechele Armstrong has done a fabulous job of creating a magical story in a short amount of pages that makes a perfect bedtime treat. 4 Angels!"

– Tammy, *Fallen Angel Reviews*

"This short story is filled with sex scenes hot enough to sizzle. Ian's surprise Christmas presents are a naughty delight that every reader will appreciate."

– Candy, *Ecataromance*

Loose Id ®

ISBN 10: 1-59632-461-9
ISBN 13: 978-1-59632-461-9
DINAH'S DARK DESIRE
Copyright © 2006 by Mechele Armstrong
Originally released in e-book format in August 2006

Cover Art by April Martinez

DISCLAIMER: Many of the acts described in our BDSM/fetish titles can be dangerous. Please do not try any new sexual practice, whether it be fire, rope, or whip play, without the guidance of an experienced practitioner. Neither Loose Id nor its authors will be responsible for any loss, harm, injury or death resulting from use of the information contained in any of its titles.

Printed in the U.S.A. by
Lightning Source, Inc.
1246 Heil Quaker Blvd
La Vergne TN 37086
www.lightningsource.com

DINAH'S DARK DESIRE

With bonus story

Dinah's Christmas Desire

Mechele Armstrong

Chapter One

Taylor Graham hesitated outside the door. He cocked his head to the side as he listened. He'd knocked twice already but there'd been no answer.

"Dinah?" he called softly, then louder. "Dinah?"

His best friend's car was parked in the lot outside the huge ground floor apartment. She hadn't shown up to their weekly lunch, nor to work that day. Calls had resulted in a busy signal at her home and no answer on her cell. He drew up his mouth in puzzlement. This wasn't like her.

If she'd been sick, she would have called work and called him. Ditto if she'd gone on a spur-of-the-moment trip. She was the responsible one. The good girl. But now where was she?

He tried the knob. It was locked.

He'd been told once upon a time not to set foot in there. But that had been by the jerk, Brad. He sighed, debating what he should do next.

His gut clenched with the inner feeling that something was wrong. No jerk's car, but Dinah's sat in the lot. They always took her car when they went together. He had to know. No one was around to give him a key, he'd already checked. He'd fix the door for Dinah later if everything was O.K.

He braced his shoulder and slammed it forward. He gave the door several good hits and kicks before the wood gave way by the lock.

"Dinah?" He pushed the door remnants open. "Dinah?"

A groan reached his ears. He stepped forward, following where he thought the sound came from.

Behind the bar in the small kitchen, Dinah lay still on the hard tile floor with the phone receiver pulled down, her arms outstretched. She'd been pulling herself toward the wayward phone.

"Dinah! Oh darling." He knelt down by her and slowly eased her onto her back. Bruises marred her pale skin, along with blood. She had a big bump on her head. "Dammit."

He grabbed the phone, quickly hung up and dialed 911. She opened her eyes as he knelt down beside her. "Taywer?"

He brushed a strand of hair back. "It's me, darling. Shhhhh." She grabbed his hand. "I'm here."

"Don...t tew. Please, don't tew..."

It took a minute to process what she was telling him. *Don't tell.*

His mouth tightened as he stroked her hand. He'd never hated anyone more than he hated Brad at that moment. Bastard.

"Shhhhh, darling. Don't talk."

He closed his eyes, fists clenching by his side. He'd watched Brad chip away at Dinah's already low self-confidence piece by piece over the last year much like Taylor chiseled wood when he carved. Brad had been an expert at it, starting slowly and working Dinah over gently at first. He'd watched him bully her into getting this apartment above both their means. Watched him push her around, push friends out of her life. Was this the first time he'd hit her? When Taylor had asked, she only said Brad loved her. Yeah, he'd loved her so much, she was now going to be in the hospital a few days. But it was the last time the asshole would get a crack at Taylor's friend. He'd see to that.

He heard the sirens in the distance as he called Ian. He needed the sound of his lover's voice. And Ian loved Dinah as much as he did. "Come to All Saint's Hospital. Dinah's been beaten."

Ian made a strangled sound. "Is she O.K.?"

"It's bad. She'll live, but he did a number on her." And he would do a number on the asshole if he ever caught him.

"Brad?" Anger laced Ian's voice. "Did you catch him?"

"No, he's not here. And he'd better be glad."

Hanging up, he held Dinah close as the paramedics came streaming into the room.

* * *

Dinah Summers sat up in the hospital bed. She stared out the windows, watching the leaves blow on the trees. A brown one blew off and floated lazily to the ground, swinging around as it fell. That was her. She was blowing in the wind, with nothing to guide her, keep her grounded. She closed her eyes, tears seeping through her lids.

Brad was gone.

His last words echoed in her mind. She'd been on the floor. "I'm leaving you for someone who can fuck. Like a real woman. You fuck worse than those fags you hang around with." His foot had lashed out again. Blinding pain had exploded in her stomach.

Shudders rocked her body as she wrapped her arms around herself, ignoring her fractured ribs. Numbness was all she could feel. All her emotions seemed muted.

What was she going to do now?

"Hey, now, none of that." Ian McNabb's musical voice skirted into the room followed closely by Taylor's deep baritone. "Yeah, none of that."

She forced a smile as her two friends surrounded her. After pulling it closer, Ian plopped in a chair right beside the bed. Taylor sat on the bed beside her, putting a firm hand on her leg. "How are you doing today?"

"I'm O.K." She bunched up the sheet in her hand. "What are you two doing here? Isn't that party tonight? Clung's, I think his name was?"

"Chip's." Ian chuckled. "And we decided we'd rather spend it with a pretty lady."

She snorted, swallowing the whimper that came up from her throat. The pain from the wounds was nothing compared to the ache she felt inside.

"It's the truth. Would I lie to you?" Taylor batted his eyelashes at her.

"Yes. Yes, you would." And she loved him for that. Luckily, they had Ian, who spoke the direct truth.

"Well, I'm not lying about that." Taylor patted her leg. "We also snuck you in a treat." He leaned in to whisper conspiratorially, "A candy bar. Had to sneak it past the nurse Gestapo." Ian slid up, giving her a peek at it from his leather jacket pocket.

Her favorite, chocolate with almonds. How was it they knew that, and Brad had never learned it the whole time they'd been together? Because Brad hadn't wanted to. The crux of it hit her hard in the stomach as it clenched. "Thanks, guys." But she couldn't prevent her eyes from filling up with new tears.

Her vision was clear enough to see that Taylor frowned, and his eyes met Ian's. He slid closer and pulled her into his arms. "I'm so glad your IV is out. I've wanted to do this ever since...ever since the first day." She still had the IV site; she'd lose that right before she left, but the bag and pole had been taken off.

Ian slid up on the bed, slipping his body as best he could around both of them. "Me, too."

She leaned into the warmth of their bodies. Taylor put one hand on her back, and so did Ian. They continually stroked up and down, their hands occasionally meeting in the middle, touching so gently that it was the barest of pressures to her ribs.

"Oh...my...I didn't mean to interrupt." The nurse on duty bustled into the room. "I need to get your stats, and you can get back to your visitors." She arched a brow at Dinah. "Your *male* visitors."

Her cheeks heated from the nurse's comment. The nurse probably thought they were freaks. How many times had Brad snapped at her for hanging around with them? Same with her father. Both said they were perverting her. Anytime she'd done anything Brad hadn't liked, he'd called her a whore. Like her father had. She'd moved from her father's house into Brad's.

She stiffened in their arms. But the loss of their warmth made her cold as they both pulled away to let the nurse take her vital signs.

"Doctor Evans is going to release you tomorrow." She eyed Taylor and Ian as she pumped up the blood pressure cuff. "Who's going to be picking you up?"

"I will," Taylor announced, standing near the chair Ian sat in.

Dinah's head came up. "You have work tomorrow."

He shrugged. "I can miss a day." He leaned back against the wall, his tall frame dwarfing the nurse's. "You'll be coming home with us."

She opened and closed her mouth a few times. "What?"

The nurse finished taking the reading. "I'll be back in a few to give you some pain medicine. Visiting hours will be up then, too." She strolled out of the room.

"You're coming home with us, Di." Taylor's voice left no room for argument.

"I can't do that. You two have your own lives..." They had their own house and had settled into it. They didn't need her hanging around.

"We've talked about it. You're moving in with us for a while." Ian's voice sounded as steely as Taylor's. His hair gleamed golden in the sunshine from the window.

Taylor's jaw tightened, and he folded his arms in front of his chest. "You're not going back to Brad."

"No. No, I'm not. He...left anyway." Somehow she'd expected to see him when she'd woken up. How on earth did she feel about that? She wasn't sure; everything was so muddled in her mind, her emotions so shoved down. Something she was used to doing.

"Good riddance." Taylor unfolded his arms and sat back down beside her. "We want you to move in. It will be fun. You're our best friend."

Dinah hesitated, picking at the sheet covering her legs. She hated the huge apartment that Brad had picked out for them. She bit her lip. The empty space would be lonely without him, too. Maybe...no, he wasn't coming back. "Won't I infringe? I mean on you two –" She paused with a heavy sigh. "– and your scenes."

Ian and Brad had been lovers for two years. While they were deeply in love, Ian was bisexual. He liked to have women, so sometimes they partied to fulfill his need. Taylor had bisexual leanings as well; he'd been with a few women before he'd discovered men. So they had fun finding a willing woman. A willing woman probably had fun with them, too.

"Not an infringement." Taylor shook his head. He ran a hand through his dark brown hair.

She and Taylor had met early in college, their freshman year. She'd been in a study group with him for a biology class. They were the only two in the group who did a damn thing. He'd been a philosophy major; she'd been an English major, living at home.

The first time she'd actually seen him, he'd been crossing the street after exercising, wearing nothing but a pair of tight biker shorts. A group of teenage girls in a pickup had come to a complete stop to whistle and scope him. Not that Dinah blamed them. He had a tight ass and legs that put runners to shame. He'd turned up the next day in her biology class. Odd, she'd never used anything that she'd learned from the class in life but they'd become fast friends, and he'd come out to her about his sexuality. Somehow that had freed her even more to talk to him about anything.

Tiredness seeped through her bones as if she were weighted down by a thousand pounds. She didn't want to argue with him, not when the idea didn't sound bad to begin with. She could lean on them awhile, linger in their friendship. "O.K. For a little while."

Taylor patted her knee. "Good."

Ian slipped the candy bar into her hand. "A little something for you." His fingers lingered on hers with the pass.

"Thanks, guys. I needed this." She'd stay with them for a week or two. Until she was back to normal. Then, figure out what she was going to do with the rest of her life.

* * *

Three months later, Dinah spread peanut butter on a sandwich and then grabbed a jar of grape jelly.

"Peanut butter is better on a warm body." Ian winked, sitting at the square wooden table, drinking his morning cup of hazelnut coffee from his "Accountants Are Sexy Numbers" cup. The sun streamed in through the windows in the open kitchen surrounded by a long bar that separated it from the living room. The light made patterns on the dark brown ceramic tile floor. She patted a white-socked foot on one of them.

"I think the office would object to that. Besides, I don't exactly have any volunteers."

"Volunteers?" Taylor stalked into the kitchen, running a hand through his wet hair. He wasn't wearing a shirt. *What a beautiful man.* He was her best friend, but even she could appreciate a view every now and again. Light splashes of dark hair peppered one well-defined, tanned chest. He worked hard every day doing carpentry, and it showed. His abs were washboard hard.

And she'd told him things she'd told no other man. Sometimes, when she became aware of him as not Taylor, her friend, but Taylor, the man, it amazed her how much she'd opened up to him. He'd always encouraged her to be freer, to express herself sexually. Next to him, she'd felt repressed, the echoes of her father's words always repeating in her brain. Of course, next to him, most people would have felt repressed. He'd had a heck of a lot of experiences.

"Volunteers to be Dinah's peanut butter sandwich." Ian's voice had turned husky, his eyes trained on Taylor, as he reached for a shirt, hanging on a wooden chair that matched the table. "No hurry covering up, you know."

Taylor grinned at him, holding the flannel shirt rather than putting it on. "I'm in no hurry. And I'd volunteer."

Dinah slapped more jelly on the sandwich, trying to ignore the gorgeousness and the lover's banter before her. "Yeah, right." She put the knife in one side of the double stainless steel sink before reaching up into the oak cabinets to get a sandwich bag.

"I would, too." Ian's emerald eyes sparkled. "I'd make a great lunch."

"Oh, yeah, you do." Taylor's eyes sparkled with mischief and desire. "We'd both volunteer for fun with peanut butter...and you."

Dinah ignored them, putting her sandwich in the plastic baggie. She didn't know how to respond when they teased in this way. And it was becoming more and more frequent.

Taylor stood behind Ian, and Ian leaned into his body as he spoke. "You know you take peanut butter every day. You could buy. Or take something different."

She shrugged, putting the baggie in her plain plastic lunch bag. "I like peanut butter."

"But variety can be a lot of fun, too." Ian smiled, showing even white teeth. His long blond hair needed a trim, but longer, it matched his personality – mischievous and smartass – more than short hair did. "Variety can be a lot of fun."

Dinah swallowed, her mouth dry. Somehow Ian wasn't only talking about her sandwich habits. "It can be. But I like peanut butter...for now."

Taylor dropped his hand on Ian's shoulder. "One day, I'll sell you on the merits of turkey."

Licking her lips, she mumbled, "I'd better get to work."

Taylor ambled over to hug her. Close to that muscular chest, she inhaled his scent. He wore some type of spicy cologne. He kissed the top of her head. "I'll be home early today."

Before he pulled away, Ian joined them, hugging her from the back. His clean scent mingled with Taylor's. Being between their bodies was warm – it had become her safe spot. She slept between them a lot of nights.

Finally, she wriggled, and they released her. "I'll see you guys tonight."

Ian kissed her cheek. "We'll get some movies for the weekend and have a movie night." Often, they went out to dinner on Fridays and got movies for the weekend. It made for fun Friday and Saturday nights, popcorn and pizza in front of the TV.

She grabbed her jacket. "That will be nice."

At work, she tossed herself into her typing and filing. Lunch was at her desk, and Karen, a friendly plump lady in the same position as her, stopped by to chat in her cubicle.

"So are you still living with those two hunks?"

Dinah nodded, eating a slice of apple. "They're my best friends." She hadn't intended to be there this long. They'd helped her break the lease on her apartment. And had moved her in with them. She'd move out soon. Or at least, stay completely out of their bed. So she kept telling herself. Most didn't know she slept with the two men sometimes. The nightmares had driven her there, even as she told everyone she was doing O.K. Ian and Taylor had become her security, her safety net. Sometimes she was scared to sleep alone.

"Oh, with friends like that…my my my." Karen smacked her lips together. "Think of being a sandwich. In the middle of all that."

Dinah shrugged, but couldn't stop an irrational twinge of jealousy over the interest of her coworker. She wasn't immune to their charms; they were both good looking guys. But she regarded them as friends. The thought of them hugging with some other woman rather than her made her heart pound. She knew they did. Taylor had talked about them being with women before she'd moved in. Ian had told Taylor that ideally he'd want to find a woman to third their relationship. Make it a permanent thing. But they hadn't had luck finding anyone. Which Dinah found hard to believe because with their looks and bodies, they should have no shortage of takers.

Lunch ended, and work began again until five. Tired on a Friday, Dinah dragged herself up the front steps. Both Ian's and Taylor's cars were home. She wondered if she could con one or both of them into a backrub.

She laid her keys where she normally left them on the counter, plunking her lunch bag in the kitchen.

Ian and Taylor weren't in the living room. She wandered, looking for them. The door to the bedroom was open, and she heard a thumping noise.

Without thinking, she stepped into the doorway. The greeting died on her lips.

Their bed faced the door so one looked at the entrance with one's head against the wooden headboard, which had shelves. Only neither Ian nor Taylor was looking. They were too busy having sex.

Taylor kneeled, with Ian thrusting into him from behind. Ian's hands cupped Taylor's shining cock, giving him a hand job even as he rammed him.

Their sweaty muscular bodies strained in time with each other.

Dinah stood, transfixed. The air whooshed out of her lungs. She couldn't turn away, couldn't move.

Taylor's huge member glistened, red and swollen, as Ian's hand went up and down along it. Taylor rocked backward with an exclamation of pleasure. His creamy semen spurted out in a long jet even as Ian didn't stop the motion of his hands nor let up in the thrusting of his body.

Her thighs clenched together, feeling suddenly slickened by moisture. Her pulse rate shot up, breathing intensifying like she'd started a run.

She could not make her legs move to back away. When was Ian going to come?

As if he'd heard her unspoken question, Ian grunted Taylor's name with two last short thrusts, collapsing against Taylor's back. Panting, they both slid down along the bed to lay together, their feet at the head, legs and arms intertwined.

She had never seen two men together, and even though she lived with them, hadn't thought much about it. But it was the most erotic thing she'd ever witnessed. Their bodies had wrapped around each other, thrusting, love and desire mingling on their faces.

Get out before they find you.

She tiptoed quickly away. Walked to the front door and slammed it. "Hey guys, I'm home!"

Taylor's voice came lazily from the back. "We'll be right there, darling."

She rubbed a hand across her face. How was she going to look them in the eye after what she'd seen? And the most horrid thought of all was that she hadn't gotten a good enough look at Ian. Taylor had told her once that Ian was bigger. After seeing Taylor, that was pretty unbelievable.

Quit thinking like that.

As she sat down on a bar stool on the other side of the counter, Taylor strolled out in black jeans that hugged his hips and no shirt. He carried the sheets.

Her face heated as he dumped them in a hamper around the corner. They'd gotten a good hosedown of Taylor's come.

"When did you get home? Ian's remaking the bed." Taylor called behind him, "Bring my shirt out when you come." He chuckled deep and low.

She turned, trying to calm down her hot face. "I just walked in the door." When she turned back, Ian had sauntered in, tossing Taylor his shirt. He wore loose khakis and a green polo shirt. Not that he'd have one so soon, but

Dinah found herself checking out between his legs for an erection. *Bigger than Taylor. Oh, my.*

Giving Taylor a knowing look, Ian mumbled something about, "...after I came." She didn't ask him to repeat it.

"Dinah *just* got home." A look she didn't recognize appeared on Taylor's face.

"Really?" Ian leaned on the other side of the counter, resting his elbows on the cool granite. "Only *just* now?"

She nodded, her teeth grazing her lip. Did they know? Know she'd been watching? She couldn't meet their eyes for fear they'd see the truth in hers or worse yet, she'd see something in theirs.

Ian dropped an arm to reach over to her with a soft hand. Warmth laced through her fingers. "You should have come earlier."

The innuendo was there, waiting for her to take it. And her mind went there, to coming. Earlier. With them.

Taylor had finished putting on his shirt, and he leaned down by Ian. "Yes, she sure should have."

This couldn't mean what she thought it meant. She swallowed, desperate to change the subject, but her mouth had dried out too much.

Ian stroked a thumb over the top of her hand. "What do you feel like having for dinner tonight?"

And Dinah cursed Karen. Because the flippant remark that came to mind was a man sandwich. The only thing was, she wasn't sure how serious she was. And would they take her up on it?

Chapter Two

Dinah popped some popcorn in her mouth, her eyes trained on the large TV. Ian reached up and nabbed her snack, munching it right out of her fingers.

"Hey, that was mine," she sputtered. "And you bit my finger." She held it up to display.

His grin slowly overtook his boyish face. "It was yours? Oh, I'm sorry. And I *nibbled* your finger. There is a difference." He leaned over, took her hand in his, and separated the offended finger from the rest, sucking it into his warm, wet mouth, rubbing his tongue across it in quick little passes. The ridged tip caressed her. "Maybe I should show you the difference."

Shifting her hips on the floor, she controlled her shudder. "Cut that out."

Taylor chuckled from the other side of her. "Does she taste as good as she looks?"

"Better." Ian's husky voice held no hint of teasing.

Dinah felt her face heat up, and she glared at them.

They both laughed, and Taylor put his arm around her shoulder as they settled back in to watch the movie. They'd pulled aside the wooden coffee table, and spread pillows and blankets in front of the dark blue sofa.

Ian slipped in closer, his muscular body against hers.

A Taylor-Ian sandwich with her in the middle.

She shivered again, telling herself to stop that. Hell, they slept together some nights with that arrangement. But more and more lately, there'd been a lot of things happening that she could almost swear were more than "friendly." She told herself not to be nuts, she'd imagined things, but they kept happening. And she didn't know how to reply.

"So do you want margaritas or daiquiris?" Taylor pushed himself to his feet.

"It doesn't matter. Whatever you want."

Taylor folded his arms in front of his chest. "Which one do you want?"

She sucked her bottom lip into her mouth. They never let her get away without making a decision. Even over something as innocuous as drinks. They made her decide bigger things, too, like what they would do over a weekend. They wanted her input on a vacation plan this summer. The trust floored her, especially with the bigger plans. What if she made a bad decision? But they always made her feel good with anything she'd decided. They said they trusted her. "Margaritas."

He did a shimmy with his hips. "Olé! I'll be right back with them."

The sound of the blender came from the kitchen and within minutes, Taylor was back with three cups of homemade margaritas. "Salty goodness."

Ian's grin had a wicked tilt to it. "You'll give me salty goodness later."

Taylor laughed heartily as Dinah stared down into the frozen concoction. Maybe she needed to sleep alone tonight? Friday and Saturday nights were two sure nights to sleep with them because she usually fell asleep in the living room. Her neck cramped with the thought of sleeping with them before weight dropped into the pit of her stomach. Taylor settled in to his position beside her.

"By the way, Di." Taylor's voice rumbled against her ear. "Your credit card bill came today."

"Hmmmm." She popped another kernel of popcorn into her mouth.

"I opened it by mistake." Ian's hand slid into hers.

She choked, her body tensing. Taylor patted her on back until she recovered her breath.

"I didn't mean to look, but by the time I realized, I already had." Ian's thumb stroked against her hand.

"It's – not that bad." A lie. She kept repeating it to herself, but she knew it wasn't true.

"You owe a helluva a lot of money. What have you been paying, the minimums?" Taylor's voice deepened.

She nodded, closing her eyes.

His hand stroked her shoulder. "Di? Did you pay for things for the asshole? Like that trip you two went on? The motorcycle he had? Even rent?"

God, she'd never intended them to find out how much debt she was in. Bad enough they already knew she'd let a jerk turn her life inside out, and then he'd left her.

"I...I didn't want you two to know. You've done so much for me already."

Now Taylor gently brushed away her hair from her face with those big hands of his. She'd seen him do his carpentry work and knew how much strength he had. And how much finesse to do little details in the woodworking he loved to do. Those strong hands would be so useful in love making.

"Darling, you should have told me. Is that the only card?"

She shook her head, feeling as miserable as a hermit crab without a shell.

Ian squeezed her hand. "How bad is it? We know how much is on that card. Are there more?"

"Bad. It's bad." And her job as an administrative assistant would never pay it off. Or at least, not in the next millennium.

"O.K. I want all the credit card bills and whatever else you have." Ian's voice sounded as businesslike as the accountant he played by day. Knowing him as well as she did, she'd never been able to imagine him in that role until now. "We'll figure out a way to get this stuff taken care of."

Dinah looked up into Taylor's blue eyes, then Ian's green ones. "I can't ask you to do that. I should get on with my life so you two can get on with yours. I've been here long enough."

"Hell, no. You aren't moving out. You could never be here long enough, Di. Ian and I agree. Right?"

Ian pulled her hand up and kissed it. His lips lingered as he spoke above her hand. "Oh, yeah."

"But…I mean, I know…I put a cramp in your love life. I should at least move out of your room permanently." Seeing what she had made her hesitant. Obviously, they found ways to have sex. But if she wasn't in there at all, they could have sex more often.

"You don't, Di." Ian's and Taylor's eyes met. A spark flashed between them. "Ian and I are doing fine with you here."

Ian released her hand and slid in, wrapping his arms around her, matching Taylor. "Bring me all your bills tomorrow. We'll work on it. And we don't want you to leave us. Not hardly."

"I don't understand why." Her voice sounded so small it made her cringe. Brad's leaving had taken away her anchor. She didn't know how to navigate anymore. Ian and Taylor had become her rudders. But soon it would be time for her to take over the controls again. She started. She'd never been at the controls. She'd never even lived on her own.

Taylor kissed the top of her head. "Because you're you."

Snuggling in, she gave in to the warmth and comfort they provided, stopping her thoughts. For now, she'd sink into the support they gave her.

* * *

Dinah drifted awake with a sleepy sigh. She stretched, laying on her side, and realized several things at once. One of them made her swallow, unsure of how to feel about it. Ian lay facing her and his hand was on her breast. A possessive hold, like a lover.

The other was usual. Taylor had spooned her back and his leg was thrown casually over hers. Every time they slept together, she woke up to Taylor's cuddly embrace in their king-sized bed.

Someone must have carried her to bed. She didn't remember coming there on her own. Last thing she did remember was snuggling in the living room watching movies and talking about her secret money problems.

She would snuggle up more to Taylor except for Ian's hand. Shifting, she tried to pull his hand off without waking him, but he tightened his hold. And slid closer to her. His leg drifted over her spread-out legs to touch Taylor's. Both men's muscular legs were encased in sweatpants. Hers were bare except for shorts. She couldn't move easily. She was effectively trapped.

Ian opened his eyes as he snuggled into her front, his bare chest against her, but keeping his hand on her chest. "Good morning."

Dinah started to say good morning, but it froze in her mouth as he began to knead her breast through Taylor's oversized t-shirt, which she'd stolen and started wearing to bed when they'd insisted she sleep with them. All the pajamas she owned were lingerie. She'd been too uncomfortable to wear those with them. They'd ceded to her presence by wearing pajama pants or sweats. She had a feeling when left to themselves, they slept naked.

She swallowed as Ian's long nimble fingers stroked around her nipple. Heat pooled low in her belly, and the nipple pebbled.

She looked into Ian's sleepy green eyes. "What are you doing?" She breathed it on a whisper. She'd aimed for a light tone but couldn't manage it. Not with him touching her.

"Playing," he answered with his rakish grin. His wavy golden hair was tousled from the night's sleep.

Before she could respond, Taylor slid closer to her back, his bare chest against her, and his large hand positioned itself on her stomach. "Good morning, Di."

"Good morning, Taylor." She breathed deeply, Ian's fingers on her nipple making it hard to think. She felt moisture build in her sex. This wasn't right. This wasn't supposed to turn her on. They were all friends.

Ian palmed her breast, squeezing it gently. Dinah's mouth went dry.

When Taylor's hand slid further down her stomach, she jumped. Ian's touch was making her skin charged. She tilted her head to look at Taylor. He smiled at her, his ebony hair shining in the low light of the morning. He brushed her hair from her eyes, and he kissed her cheek at the same time his hand breached her underwear.

"Taylor," she gasped, as his hand slid into her slick wetness. One finger delved in to find how creamy she was, how much this was making her burn. That should have embarrassed her but didn't. She couldn't think with them touching her about why this was wrong. All she could do was let the sensations take her. It needed to stop, but she couldn't express it. Or even say why.

His eyes shut, and he growled low and deep in his throat. "God, Di." His finger parted her folds and flicked her nub. Her hips arched up in pleasure. "Your clit's so hard." Taylor panted.

She moved her leg slightly, and it came into contact with his erection.

That brought her back to this needing to stop. She couldn't let it continue. "Taylor...this isn't..."

Taylor continued as Ian lowered his head and took her nipple into his hot wet mouth through the t-shirt. His tongue flicked back and forth along it. He rocked his hips against her leg, and she felt his hardness against her.

"Ohhhhh," she moaned and tried to get some reason into her brain, which was being assaulted by sensations. "Oh, god..." she tried again.

Taylor stilled, but didn't remove his fingers, and Ian didn't stop but continued to suckle her through the shirt.

"Do you trust me?" Taylor whispered and lightly swirled one finger around her. She writhed, the barely-there touch making her want more, want it harder. Her breath caught in her throat as she tried to focus on what he said. His blue eyes looked intently into hers. "Do you trust Ian?"

Ian lifted his head, removing his mouth from her breast, but his hand came up to pinch the nipple.

"Yyyyyyesss," she stammered out, still caught in the web of desire, her mind not working well. "I trust you...but..."

"I won't do anything you don't want me to," he whispered. "If you want me to stop, I'll stop. Tell me no, and it ends. But right now, I don't think that's what you want." Taylor wiggled one finger around her folds, causing new moisture to flood into his fingers. He and Ian eased her completely onto her back from her side. "Your body is telling me you want this to continue. Let yourself go, Di. Completely. We'll take this slow."

Ian tugged on her shirt, pulling it up. "Trust us. We won't push you for more yet. But let us make you feel good right now." He yanked her shirt up to her neck and looked down with a wicked gleam at her bared chest. "Beautiful. You are so beautiful, Dinah."

She shivered at the look in his eyes and at the longing in his voice. He must be crazy. They were both beautiful. Doubt ate away at the desire. "They're too small." She closed her eyes.

"Open your eyes, Dinah. Look at me."

She raised her eyelids open slowly.

"You have the firmest breasts. Such large, sensitive nipples." He flicked one, and she shivered. Taylor's hand was hit with another wave of moisture. "They're beautiful. Makes me want to eat them all up."

Ian eagerly latched onto a nipple, suckling and teasing it with his tongue and wet mouth. His ministrations had her arching up her pelvis. Or maybe it was Taylor's fingers delving deeper and deeper into her tight channel, stretching her, and fingering her nub with his thumb.

Dinah felt her orgasm building, banking and swirling her in its intensity. Taylor captured her mouth with his to kiss her deeply, and when his tongue touched hers, she exploded, her hips arching her sweet spot wildly into Taylor's hand. He let her rock against him and kissed her until her shudders finally stopped. Ian didn't stop until her climax ended.

They both looked down at her with eyes full of pride and said in unison, "Good morning, Dinah." Ian kissed her gently, his tongue probing her mouth while Taylor pulled his hand out of her. He stretched himself out lazily as the kiss with Ian finished.

Dinah swallowed, her breathing starting to slow. Her hands shook. She pushed them away slowly. "What…why?" She huffed, her breath halting in her throat. "Why did you two do that?" Incredible – her bliss had known no bounds. Her stomach jittered. She looked to the high cathedral ceiling, avoiding looking in the eyes of the men who'd jointly brought her to climax. When Ian spoke, she lowered her eyes.

"Because we all wanted it." Ian leaned back in the bed, stretching out to his bare toes. A bulge stood out in the beige sweatpants he wore. That made her look to Taylor even as Ian spoke. A bulge stood evident there, too. They'd given her pleasure and hadn't taken their own. Their hard-ons were proof of that. No man had ever taken her over the edge without coming himself. Well, Brad, the only man she'd been serious with, hadn't, nor had her first lover from prom night in high school. Her hand clenched in confusion. "And you needed it."

Taylor put a rough hand on her still shaking one. "You needed it. And so did we."

She pushed the dark blue spread off the bed, baring it to the light blue sheets, shaking off Taylor's hand. "It wasn't right."

"Why not?"

"Because it...wasn't." Her chaotic thoughts wouldn't form logical sentences. She had always thought of herself as a "one man at a time" woman. As she moved, moisture pooled between her thighs and oozed. Her heartbeat zipped along. She couldn't deny what they did had turned her on. And that should bother her, shouldn't it?

Ian chimed in. "You enjoyed it. What's wrong with that?"

"I...I don't know." She clenched a thigh under her hand. "Ian. Taylor. This is nuts."

"Darling." Taylor didn't touch her, but he shifted closer to her as though he wanted to. "It's not nuts. We're all adults. No one was hurt. And it's something we've wanted to talk to you about."

"We were waiting for you to be ready." Ian's head bobbed up and down. "To be strong enough after what happened."

"Ready for what?" She swallowed through a dry throat. It couldn't be what she thought.

"Ready to come into our relationship."

"What?" It was what she'd thought. Though she'd been expecting it, to hear it aloud sent her thoughts fumbling over each other. "You're serious?"

Taylor's eyes bored into hers. His face tightened soberly. "Very much so."

"Me?"

"There's no one else we'd like more. We both love you already."

Now Ian scooted closer to Taylor. "And in case you hadn't noticed, we find you extremely attractive." He looked her up and down.

Dinah looked down at her body. She'd always seen herself as pudgy, small-breasted. Brad always said... She shook her head. She wasn't going to think in terms of what Brad said. Never again. It was something she was working on at Taylor and Ian's urging. Same with things her father had said about her. She'd talked to her father only once since Brad had left only for him to rail against her loose ways. Sadly, she hadn't missed their conversations. "Me?" she repeated.

"You." Taylor put an arm behind Ian, who leaned into him. They presented a united front, which made it that more disconcerting. They'd already discussed this. They knew what they wanted with her.

"I can't do this."

"Don't say no yet."

"Don't." Ian echoed Taylor.

Taylor continued, "Give us time to show you what this arrangement can be like. Time to convince you, this can be good for all of us."

"Time for us to woo you." Ian's smile lit his whole face.

"Woo? I don't know about all this. How much time?" The words came out before she could stop them. What the hell was she doing? Nice girls didn't get involved with threesomes. No matter how good friends they were with the boys. Or how hot the boys were. Or how they'd given her the longest orgasm without batteries she'd ever had.

"I don't know, couple of weeks?" Taylor looked at Ian for affirmation.

"A couple of weeks," Ian said, reiterating. "At least. Let us get to know you, and you get to know us. Let us show you what this arrangement can be like."

"How do you know what's it like?" She scratched her cheek, stalling. She loved them both. But taking them both sexually at the same time had never seriously entered her mind. She was a good girl, who wanted to be married some day. Have a family. Threesomes didn't do that. Did they? Not anything she'd ever researched before.

The breakup with Brad must have hit her even harder than she'd thought, if she was even considering this.

"Because I've known people in this kind of relationship. And it's what I've been looking for. For myself and Taylor."

"Oh." He knew people in this kind of thing. Maybe it wasn't as abnormal as it seemed to her. Who was she kidding? The picket fence image never involved Dick, Rob, and Jane.

Taylor reached over to stroke her cheek, giving her a contrite look as though he couldn't help himself. She could smell herself on his fingers, making her body shiver in remembrance, not that she'd ever forget what they'd done. It was etched across her mind for all time. "We realized some time ago, the reason we couldn't find anyone to come into our relationship was because there was only one person we wanted. *You.*"

She closed her eyes, then slid off the bed. She turned to face them. They both looked so hopeful, sitting near the headboard. And so...yummy. She did love them. They were her best friends. They even knew when she went on the rag down to the day. Taylor showed up with her favorite double chocolate ice cream. Maybe transitioning to something more wouldn't be that hard. "I'll think about it."

It was all she could say, and she couldn't even believe she meant it. She reached up to put a hand on her head. Maybe she was ill. That would explain her muddled thoughts.

Ian smiled so wide, his even white teeth peeked out against his lips. "That's all we're asking."

"Oh, yeah. Now come back to bed, darling." Taylor patted the spot by him, then crooked a finger at her.

"Why?" She eyed them both suspiciously. Did they want another round of making out? They must want something; they hadn't been satisfied.

"Because it's Saturday. We don't have to be up yet. It's not even nine." Oh, it was Saturday. They slept in every weekend.

Slowly, she walked back to the bed. Somehow the idea of the Christians facing the lions in Rome came to mind. Only these two lions would make the eating feel wonderful. She staved off a shiver at the thought.

She must have been taking too long. Ian and Taylor both started laughing. "We aren't going to roast you." Taylor shook his head.

"Or eat you. Yet, anyway." Ian raised his brows at her. Damn, the man was good, zeroing in on her thoughts like he'd read them.

"Seriously." Taylor touched Ian lightly on the shoulder, shaking his head. "We only want to cuddle."

She lifted herself onto the foot of the bed and slid in between them. It didn't feel uncomfortable. The warm of their bodies brushed hers. Her safe spot had become in between them. And what had happened this morning hadn't changed that. She curled up, Taylor wrapping an arm around her.

"Watch the wet spot." Ian snickered as the heat rose in her cheeks again. Taylor smacked him lightly across the back of the head with his other hand. "Hey, it is wet."

"Shut up and go back to sleep." Taylor wrapped her firmly into his arms. Ian snuggled up into them.

She drifted off to sleep thinking about what she'd agreed to and wondering if it was the right decision.

* * *

The next day, Taylor watched as Dinah painted her toenails a vivid shade of pink. She sat on the floor of their bedroom. His eyes followed the curve of her calf. Her head tilted down, dark hair hanging around it like a curtain. Even her feet were rounded, beautifully arched. She had small toes. She concentrated, her tongue shooting out between her lips, taking a swipe, then plunging back in.

His erection jerked.

Funny, how you could know a woman for so many years, but once carnal thoughts became standard, they never stopped.

Meeting in college, he and Dinah had kept a constant friendship, even when he'd come out to her. So put down all her life, he found that her pluck had endured, which he loved about her. It needed encouragement, but it was there. She'd become more than a friend long ago. And his interest in her as more than even that had been piqued right before Brad had come into the picture. One minute, Dinah had been planning to move out from under her father's rule, and the next, she'd ended up under Brad's. Damn the asshole, his timing and his fists especially. Brad better hope Taylor never ran into him again.

He took a step forward, and a creak sounded on the wooden slats of the hardwood. They had a carpet remnant installed under their bed, sticking out about four feet from it, but from there to the walls, to the master bath, and to the door was all hard wood. Ian didn't enjoy cold floors under his feet in the mornings so the carpet was a concession to him. Taylor liked hard wood. In more ways that one.

Her head swiveled around to look at him, hair falling back. "Oh, hi, Taylor."

"Hey, darling." He sat beside her, tilting himself enough sideways to see her face, putting one hand on her hunched back. "How are you doing?"

"Loverly." She swiped one last time down her little toenail. "Damn, I smeared it." She rubbed the paint off with her thumb.

"You should go get a pedicure. A manicure. Make it a spa day." He leaned back against the bed. He'd made the headboard and footboard out of oak with shelves and intricate carvings of vines, then lightly stained it, as a present to Ian.

Her head shook back and forth. "Nah. I can paint them myself. I'll save that for another time." Left unsaid was the money issue. They'd worked to set up payment schedules with the credit card companies and made a couple of deals.

Quietness reigned between them. Not normal for them. She always told him everything.

He watched her through half-closed lids. Like hell this would go on. They'd always talked, not chatted. He wouldn't let her hide from this, from him. "So we surprised you the other morning." They hadn't talked about it, and they hadn't pushed her for more. Yet.

The flush crept up her cheeks like some red river. "I think you know you did."

"It wasn't our intention." It hadn't been. She was doing so well with what had happened, they'd hoped it was time. He shrugged his shoulders. "It was mentioned before, you know. To you."

Her eyes widened. "When?"

"A movie night. A long time ago. *Casablanca.*" Everything about that night had remained oddly clear in his mind.

Comprehension dawned on her face. "I'd forgotten all about that. And I had no idea you were serious."

They'd been having an evening get together at Taylor's apartment where they watched old movies, ate dinner and lots of popcorn, much like the movie nights they had now. *Casablanca* was the first movie they'd watched that night. She'd found out Ian was bisexual. The conversation had continued after the movie finished.

"One day –" Ian had leaned back on the pillows. "– I'd like to find a woman. An open-minded woman. That way I can have the best of both." Ian liked consistency. He wanted both a steady man and woman to be with.

"I'm sure you'll find someone." She had picked at some nonexistent lint on the floor, her face impassive. Taylor and Ian both had closely monitored her reactions.

"How about you? You interested?" Ian's voice hadn't changed inflection but when Taylor had looked at him, Ian's eyes wouldn't meet his. He'd sucked his lip between his teeth. A sure sign he'd been serious.

Taylor hadn't considered Dinah with more than a passing thought until that moment. But it made so much sense, had a certain rightness to it.

Awkwardness had reigned for a minute until Taylor waggled his brows. Her eyes had sought his. She adored Ian, his lover, as her friend, but then, had still been more comfortable with Taylor. She'd known him longer.

"Oh, no." She had shaken her head with a nervous chuckle. "I'm a one woman, one man kind of girl."

"If you ever change your mind..." Ian's eyes had bored into hers. "Let us know."

"Yeah, you don't even have to audition," Taylor had joked.

No more had ever been said. Two days after that, she had met the asshole, Brad. Who knew what would have happened had she not.

Taylor sighed. "I'm not sure how serious we were back then." Though they had been, a little. "But, it didn't matter. You met Brad. We're very serious now."

She looked down at her feet as if they were the most interesting thing in the world. "I made a big mistake with Brad."

He swirled his fingers in circles around and around her back with the arm he had put around her. She groaned softly as his thumb found her spine, pressing on it through her t-shirt. "Are your nails dry?"

Without moving her head, she said, "Probably."

"Lay down." Cracking his knuckles, he moved away from her so she could stretch out.

She shot a dubious look at him. But did as he'd asked.

Her long body lay on the carpeted floor. She was clothed simply in jeans and a t-shirt, but his heart still quickened at her laid out for him. Maybe one day she'd be his banquet. But for today, he was going to give her some spa time, Taylor style.

His hands worked hard during the day. Ian told him if ever quit construction, he'd have a future as a masseur. Course, Ian also said the same thing about him being a porn star. Not a good thought with Dinah on the floor in front of him. She'd be quite the star.

He reached up into his dresser and pulled out some almond massage oil. Squirting a little out on his hands, he warmed it between his fingers. It would be easier if she took off her shirt, but she'd not be comfortable with that. And this was for her, so he'd work around it.

Sliding the shirt part way up her back, he pressed a palm into the small of her back, spiraling around in the slippery oil.

She swallowed loudly, and her body remained tense.

"Relax. It's me. Taylor." It was the first time he'd given her a massage on the bare skin of her back, but not the first massage. He'd rubbed her neck a few times when it ached.

Under her shirt, he kneaded up her back, slightly surprised to find she wore no bra. He hadn't noticed; he must be slipping.

Her breasts were loose, unbound. They pressed into the floor. He should have checked them out more when she'd been upright. Course, he had seen the bare thing that morning with Ian. Nothing compared to that. He swallowed, shifting his weight around, his hips swiveling on the floor.

After a few minutes of massaging, her body relaxed, lying limply. He pressed on the points of her spine, twiddling his finger into each crevice.

She moaned, the hoarse sound coming from deep within. It moved her skin under his fingertips.

His mouth went dry, though he kept up his actions. Would she sound like that when she agreed to come into the threesome and took them both? Such a throaty sound. Could they make her scream? Ian would try. His cock bumped against his zipper. Face down, she couldn't see his arousal.

He repeated a list of vegetables to keep his mind off the softness of her skin. The roundness of her curves. And the soft petal scent of flowers that spilled into the air from her whenever she walked into a room.

Right after he'd discovered men, he'd been much more into his own gender. But, then, Ian had come into his life and re-introduced him to the joys of having a woman. He'd had them before but never like he did with Ian. How women trembled. How they got wet under fingertips. How their pussies opened like the petals of an iris. He'd read that somewhere, and it had always stuck with him.

He passed a hand along her lower back, grazing her fine ass. "Better? As good as a spa?"

Her muffled voice rose up from the floor. "Oh, yeah. I think you're going to need a shovel to get me off the floor. I'm a puddle."

He closed his eyes, imagining her after they'd had their way with her. Limp. Sweaty. Sated. *Not a puddle yet. But you will be.*

Chapter Three

Three days later, Dinah tapped on the collision balls desk toy that rested on her desk. It rattled as the balls hit each other. She let out a sigh.

It was almost lunchtime. She'd been running around all morning without a moment to think. Each time she did stop for a minute, she had the same thoughts running around her head.

She was enjoying herself with Taylor and Ian.

She could tick off a big list why. They were fun and made her laugh. They listened to her, not making her feel stupid, letting her make decisions on her own and trusting them. They made her feel like a woman, sexy and feminine. They were everything that she'd ever imagined in a partner.

So what was wrong with that?

They were more than she'd ever imagined in a partner. They were "they" and not one man.

She'd always imagined her life with a husband, getting married, kids, the all-American dream. Never had she imagined being part of a threesome.

Until now.

But the doubts crept in to make her hesitate.

Good girls had one man at a time.

It was easy to become a whore. A slut.

Was it wrong to have two? Hell, was it greedy? Why did one woman need two guys?

She'd heard a girl in college once refer to a threesome woman as "one greedy bitch." Women would love to get their hands on Ian or Taylor separately. Her eyes told her that much when they all went out. She'd seen so many craned necks to get a look at those two. The two together were a powerhouse no sexual woman could resist.

And she could have them both if she wanted them. They'd made that clear. All she would have to do was agree.

What should she do?

"The thoughts look worth more than a penny. Maybe a nickel?" Karen grinned as Dinah startled at her approach into Dinah's cubicle on black high heels. "Must be thinking about those guys you've got at home. You know you could share one of 'em. Not be so greedy." Though it was teasing, there was a hard edge to the comment.

Dinah cleared off some papers by the metal conference seat Karen flopped down in. Too ironic Karen should make that comment now.

Dinah picked up her lunch bag from where it lay on the floor under her desk. It was thermal, and she rarely brought cold things. She put it by her desk every day when she came in. "Sure am. Why don't you have lunch here today? We can talk."

Karen's smile was enough to make Dinah feel guilty for not doing it every day. She shifted her feet under her desk, and moved some more papers. The zipper of her bag clinked on the cold fake wood veneer as she slid it across to make way for the stuff she'd moved out of Karen's way.

"Eating lunch at your desk today?" Karen had a salad from the office cafeteria in her hand with two packets of a reddish dressing. Probably about the safest thing to eat from there. She flipped her blond hair over one shoulder. Her heavy breasts bounced under her red sweater with the motion of getting settled in the chair.

As she pulled out her sandwich baggie, something tickled Dinah's fingertips. She looked down to see a big fat roach scramble out of the bag and onto her fingers.

"Aieyeeeeee!" She flung the bug into the air over the low cubicle walls, pushing back from her desk in a panic. "Oh, ewwwwwwwwwwwwwwww." That thing had been in with her sandwich. She could still feel its little feet running over her hand.

"Gross." Karen wrinkled up her nose, springing open her plastic salad container. She pulled out a fork from plastic wrap and started to eat.

Dinah gulped, trying not to watch Karen take bites. How could she eat after seeing the pest? Retaking her seat, she looked carefully all over her lunch bag. Nothing else was in it that she could see. She stuffed all her food and lunch bag in the trash can. Her hunger had disappeared with the bug.

"You ought to report that to maintenance. That's icky." Karen crunched into a big piece of lettuce.

"I will, don't worry. I had no idea that there were roaches in here." Dinah shivered, her body rocking back and forth, trying not to think about what could have happened. She could have eaten some of her food before she discovered it. That would have made her sick. Roaches produced big ick and fear reactions in her. They had ever since childhood, when she'd once been locked in an old closet crawling with roaches. Her father had laughed when he'd finally let her out.

"I haven't heard anything about a roach infestation." Karen paused in her munching. "That's a new one to me."

"Really?" Dinah leaned back in her desk chair, a spring creaking. "That was a huge roach." Hadn't her baggie been shut? She had closed it this morning. Maybe jostling had opened it. She'd been away from her desk off and on all morning. Not that she would have noticed a bug climbing into the lunch bag. She hated cockroaches. She rubbed at her arms. It would be time for a shower as soon as she got home.

"I haven't heard anything about it." Karen was the office center point of gossip, so she would have.

"Must be a new infestation." Dinah opened each and every one of her desk drawers, peeking in them for bugs as Karen finished her lunch.

* * *

Ian set his keys down by Dinah's. He liked the intimacy of her living with him and Taylor. Clothes washed together in the washer. Her bath stuff sitting with theirs on the sink. He couldn't wait until it was all settled and permanent. No doubts existed that eventually she'd find her way to them.

Taylor was working late, doing a big job. His philosopher turned carpenter, Taylor had gone back to his first enjoyment after he'd graduated, woodworking and carpentry. With him working late, that left Ian and Dinah alone. Time for him to work on winning Dinah over.

One finger stroked her keys. She was so much like him, a creature of habit in so many ways. If only Taylor would leave his in the same place, he wouldn't lose them so often. His silly lover. Thinking of Taylor always brought a smile. And a hard-on.

"Dinah?" he called softly. He didn't want to startle her. "Dinah?"

She didn't answer. A few paces to the bottom of the steps, he heard the sounds of a shower. She sometimes took one when she got home. Like he did.

An image of her lush curves covered in water and soap running down them flashed in his mind. Blood surged to his cock. He could join her. Make sure she got everywhere clean. Especially her delicate folds in her precious pussy.

He joined Taylor in the shower often. Taking Taylor or oral sex was a great way to start off the day. Both was even better.

He kicked off his shoes where he normally left them, by a dusty blue recliner in the living room.

She wasn't ready. A freakout would be her reaction to his joining her.

A long sigh blew deep from his lungs. He'd wait for her to be ready. No matter how many showers and bars of soap it took for him to keep control.

Stalking down the hall, he went to their bedroom, the water sounds intensifying. She often used the shower in their master bathroom. He'd given Taylor a blowjob in there that morning. His cock twitched, much the way it had as he'd enveloped his lover's cock with his mouth, swirling his tongue around and suctioning.

To think that when Dinah had first moved in, they'd tried celibacy. It hadn't lasted a day. They both liked their slap and tickle too much. So ingenious ways of getting together had been had. Dinah never seemed to notice when one of them disappeared, and the other was in the shower. Or, if she did, she didn't say anything.

He laid on the bed, his cock pressing into the sheets, waiting for Dinah to get out of the shower. His hips angled downward. He was horny as hell. Maybe he should go find a shower in another bedroom and jerk off. But he wanted to see her, spend some time without Taylor there. They didn't get a lot of time with only the two of them.

Lying on his back, closing his eyes, Ian remembered the night he'd come out to her as bi. People had rejected him for enjoying both sexes. He'd gotten quite jaded about it and expected her to run screaming from the room. Because apparently liking both men and women was akin to being a murderer in some people's eyes, or at least he would say that from the reactions he received.

They'd been watching *Casablanca*. She'd sighed a bit dreamily at the end of the movie. "Humphrey Bogart is such a hero as Rick."

Taylor had laughed. "I told you. It's a great movie." Neither of them could believe she hadn't seen it already.

Ian had taken a swig of his beer, leaning back against the couch and stretching out his legs. "Yep, Bogart is a definite A-list guy. But boy, Ingrid Bergman is a beautiful woman. Such a gorgeous face. Rrrrrr," he'd purred. And scanned Dinah's face to gauge her reaction.

At that time, Dinah had been more important to Taylor. They'd known each other longer. But he'd had a secret crush on Taylor's best friend. Her rejection would cost.

Dinah's eyes had narrowed as she stared at Ian, but she hadn't asked. Typical Dinah. She'd come out of her shell so much living with them, but back then, she'd been even more reserved.

Taylor had caught her eye. "Did I mention Ian's bi?" Taylor had been dating Ian for a couple of months. But he hadn't brought things up to Dinah yet about that. Ian had decided to push the issue. He wanted her to know, wanted to be important to her.

"Bi?"

"I'm bisexual. I like men and women." Ian had looked at her, daring her to reject him. As so many had.

But she hadn't. She'd come to accept him as warmly as she did Taylor.

Making his crush grow by leaps and bounds.

"Ian," a voice whispered. "Are you awake?"

Relaxed on the lull of his sleepy state, he sighed, turning over. His eyes peeked open to see Dinah's face peering curiously at him. "Sort of." Her hair draped over her shoulders, wet and a little drippy. He wanted to fist his hands into it. Stroke them through the silken strands. It was dark like the night, like Taylor's hair and tanned body. Most of his favorite things involved darkness. He shook off the sleepiness, trying to get himself aware.

She giggled. "You look so cute when you're sleeping." It was the first time since Brad had come into her life that he'd seen happiness replace the shadows in her eyes.

"Did you watch me sleep?" He pushed up on one elbow on the large full-body pillow.

She shrugged, moving away to pick up a brush from on top of the dresser she shared with Taylor. "Maybe."

"Did I drool? Did I snore?"

Her laugh rolled out from between her shoulder blades. "I didn't see any drool. But you snore. Softly, though."

He stretched out his limbs. The stupor still clutched him, but was slowly lifting. "Unlike the buzz saw. Taylor could wake the dead." When he rolled on his back, his love had a nasty snore. Ian had to wake him up sometimes.

"Oh my god! He can sure snore, can't he?" Facing him, she raised the brush and began pulling it through her tresses. She winced at a tangle.

"Here." Ian sat up and patted the bed in front of him. "Let me help."

She eyed him dubiously.

"Come on. I can get out a few tangles. I used to date a hairdresser so I know all about brushing hair." He patted the sheet again. "Afterwards, you can sit on Santa Ian's lap and tell him whether you've been good or bad." He winked at her. "I'm voting bad. Very bad."

She snorted. "I'm a good girl." Tiptoeing to the bed, she then sat down in front of him. "But I'll let you help brush my hair. It needs to be cut, it's tangling something awful."

He took the purple brush from her small hands. He ran the bristles through her hair, taking great care not to pull too hard. Dinah was too much of a good girl. It was their biggest hurdle to cross with her coming into the relationship.

He used sure, even strokes to get all the tangles from her hair, stroking through the soft strands with the other hand.

Her breathing grew deep and rhythmic. He continued to brush long after he'd gotten out the tangles, gliding the bristles through the hair with a light touch.

His free hand moved from her hair to her neck, squeezing around the tight muscles down near her shoulders. He used his pointer finger to zero in on the bumps of her spine.

"Ohhhh." Her moan echoed in the bedroom. Her head jerked up as though the sound surprised her. "Oh, thank you, Ian. Thanks a lot." She scooted over to the edge and put her hands down to push off.

He grasped her shoulders before she could get leverage to get up. "Ah, ah, ah. No getting up yet." He pulled her backwards, relying on a hope she wouldn't resist. She didn't. She was so petite, so little. Of course, his other lover was huge, at least four inches taller than his own six feet, much wider and much more muscular. So her five-foot-six frame would seem small. She felt so dainty, so light. "You're a feather."

"Ha ha. I'm –"

His fingers left her shoulder to shoot one hand around and tap one finger on her lips. Never would she talk bad about herself in his presence. Yet another thing he wanted to punch Brad for. "You're not fat. You have curves, unlike twiggy little models." He pulled her onto his lap the rest of the way.

She swallowed. It traveled down her body, making a gulping sound. Sitting in his lap, she had to feel his hard-on. It pressed against her cute rounded ass.

Sweeping the hair to the side, he leaned in to press a kiss on her cheek. "Yes, your curves are attractive. They attract me." He wiggled his hips, making his erection even more obvious.

Slowly, he kissed up her neck, nibbling the spot below her ear. Her breath blew out of her lungs. He reached her earlobe, turning her sideways so he could have access.

"Ian…" She closed her eyes as if seeking strength. Reopening them, she spoke, "I don't know about this." Her body remained tense.

He blew softly into her ear. She shook her head, a giggle breaking out of her closed mouth. "I won't push you for more. You can keep your clothes on. Give it a chance." He bit his lip. He wanted her so badly. She needed time to adjust to the new aspect of their relationship, but it was so hard to give that when all he could think about was how good it would feel to have her sandwiched between him and Taylor.

How good it would feel to share her with his lover. It was his dream to have a lover who was permanent, who there was an emotional attachment to, rather than the one nights they'd been doing.

"I don't know."

He nipped her earlobe, eliciting a shiver. She shifted her thighs. *You want this.* He'd bet if he dipped into her pussy, he'd find her primed and ready. That spurred him on. If he even suspected she didn't like what he was doing or felt truly uncomfortable, he'd stop. His tongue traced her lobe, skirting up the shell of it to dive into a crevice at the top. His arm encircled her, bringing her tighter against him.

As his tongue explored her ear, he breathed deeply. The scent of her hair was sweet, almost flowery. The fresh scent of her body wash lingered, something with a musky undertone.

Her body trembled in his lap, causing his cock to jerk with the motion against it.

He explored the base of her neck again, nipping. Twisting his hips, he pushed to the side to lay her down in the bed beside him.

"Ian."

"Clothes stay on. But I want to do the other side, and I couldn't reach it with you sitting on my lap."

He licked a path up the other side of her neck, finding her ear and exploring it much the same as he had the first. But when he got to the ear canal, he pressed his tongue, in and out, in and out. He created a rhythm much like what he wanted to do with his cock. Her hips jerked. He placed one leg in between her thighs, encouraging her to wrap around it, to squeeze it. With a whimper, she did so, riding his leg with thrusts against it.

His mouth left her ear to slide against her mouth. Gently and lightly, he kissed her, slowly deepening the kiss to a full one.

He almost lost his resolve when her tongue shyly sought his. It twirled around, dancing. With a moan, he shot his tongue into her mouth much as he'd done to her ear, creating an in and out motion.

Her eyes darkened when he pulled away. Her hair was spread out on the pillow, her pale cheeks had colored with a pink flush. Her chest rose and fell quickly with the short spurts of breathing she was doing. She licked her swollen lips, her tongue that had been dueling with his sliding only part way out.

Oh, the things that little motion brought to mind.

With a deep breath, he managed a smile and forced his control. She was worth the wait. "What do you want for dinner, Di?"

"What?" Her face clouded with confusion.

"Dinner. Tell me what you want, and I'll fix it."

"Oh." She lay quietly against him for a few more seconds. "You aren't going to push me, are you?"

"Not until you're ready. I already told you that." His aching cock would have to suffer for a while. He'd rather give up now and win, than take it and lose.

"Most guys…"

He rubbed her arm, gently scraping his knuckles up the velvety skin. "I'm not most guys. Neither is Taylor. And you've only had one serious relationship. Don't color all guys with Brad's brush."

"Where is Taylor?" She shifted her body away from him, not breaking the touch of their bodies, but limiting it.

"He's working late. It will be you and me." Ian smiled, wicked thoughts crossing his mind.

"Oh, that's right. He mentioned that. What?" She ducked her head almost down to her chest, scanning his face.

"In some traditions, when a Scottish man found his mate, he'd feed her from his plate. I did that for Taylor the night I asked about us moving in together." It had been a phenomenal night. They'd fucked relentlessly for hours on end. Taylor had topped him, not a position he usually took.

The desire must have shown on his face because Dinah smiled. "That must have been quite a night."

Ian nodded. "When you decide to officially make the commitment, Taylor and I will feed you. We've already talked about it." It would be another wonderful night. He'd watched Dinah slowly recover from what Brad had done to her. The physical damage had been easy. But the emotional damage still lasted. She was better, so much stronger, but still had growing to do. And he couldn't wait until she was theirs.

"When?" She arched an eyebrow at him.

"When." He nodded. "I mean, what's not to love?" He grinned, waggling his brows at her.

"You're so arrogant." Choking out a laugh, she sat up.

Laughing with her, he took her hand and got up. "Let's go get dinner going. How was your day?"

"Good. Except for the great big roach!"

Chapter Four

Dinah ran a finger over the shelf of comedy DVDs at the movie store. Decision time for a movie. They each picked one every week. Ian's tastes ran to horror movies, Taylor's to suspense. And she loved a light comedy or romance.

She decided on a movie and dashed to find Ian. She was usually the first one finished. Taylor always took his time.

Cruising into the horror section, the usual tease about women being the ones who were supposed to take forever died on her lips as she rounded the end of the aisle. Ian leaned back against a shelf, chatting rather exuberantly to a woman, who stood in front of him.

The woman reached out and touched his arm. He smiled instantaneously, leaning into her.

Dinah bit her lip, surveying the situation, sizing up the woman who Ian knew and was rather comfortable with.

Long willowy blond hair floated down her back past thin hips to a shapely butt. Tall and slender, she turned, brushing back her hair. Her jeans hugged her hips like a second skin below a purple scoop neckline top that didn't quite meet the top of them, showing her belly button. Her face was long and angular, cat eyes gleaming from above a pug nose. Even under the harsh fluorescent lights that made Dinah appear pallid, this woman was stunning. And something about her seemed familiar.

Ian noticed her standing at the end of the aisle. He smiled warmly, motioning her to come forward. "Di. Sorry, I didn't notice you standing there."

"Oh, this is Dinah?" Her eyes met the woman's. And the woman did as much sizing her up as Dinah'd done a minute ago. "I've heard a lot about you." Her deep voice resonated in the space.

Dinah nodded. "I'm Dinah. And you are?" She didn't want to say she'd heard nothing about her so she ignored the other woman's comment.

Ian grinned, a little sheepishly. "Ah, sorry. This is Caitlin."

Caitlin touched his arm. "You never were good at this formal stuff. Call me, Cait, Dinah. It's good to finally meet you." She didn't offer her hand to be shaken. Instead, she clutched Ian's elbow with pink-painted, manicured long nails.

Dinah shoved her short stubby unpainted fingernails down by her side. She licked her lips. "Good to meet you. How –"

Taylor interrupted, lumbering up, movie in hand.

"Hey, guys, I found a –" Taylor stopped short as Dinah moved to the side so he would see Cait. "Cait." A chill laced through his voice. Dinah's eyes jumped between Ian and Taylor. And then to Cait. Ian stiffened, his eyes narrowing at Taylor's one word. She hadn't imagined the coldness. Ian's reaction told her that.

Who was Cait? And why did Taylor have a strong reaction to her? Had they had sex with her? She frowned. Intimacy existed with Ian and Cait. That much was obvious.

"It's been a while, Taylor." Cait's hand moved up onto Ian's bicep. Her fingers tightened with a possessive hold.

"Yeah. It has." Taylor's face hardened.

Cait's honeyed voice continued, "But I'm glad I ran into you. I've been wanting to meet Dinah." Cait's head swiveled to look at her.

Taylor placed an arm around her shoulders. "This is *our* Dinah."

Cait arched a brow above her golden eyes, her eyebrows going up under the matching bangs.

"Taylor, did you finally find a movie?" Ian's usually tender smile seemed harsh and didn't quite reach his eyes. Dinah leaned into Taylor, absorbing his warmth in the chilly store. Course it wasn't chilly because of the temperature controls. In all the time they'd been together, she'd never seen them seriously have an argument. But something was up tonight.

"Sure did." Taylor held up a box with his other hand. His features didn't have the usual teasing lightheartedness. "Right here."

Ian clucked his tongue. "*The Bourne Identity?* We've seen it."

"Yeah. But it's good." Taylor's fingers gripped the box tighter. His muscles flexed around Dinah as he straightened.

"I don't want to see it again." Ian folded his arms across his chest. Cait's hand went with his. She wasn't letting go of him.

"Something else you'd prefer?" Taylor's teeth gritted together. Ian had never objected to a movie pick before. Taylor didn't usually get things they'd seen before, but Dinah had.

"Something I haven't seen." Ian showed his own black case, unfolding his arms. "Dinah? What did you get?"

Her tongue gingerly moistened her lips again. "*Bedazzled.*" She'd gotten a new-to-her movie, but now wished she'd gotten something familiar. She didn't understand why Ian had reacted as he had.

Ian waved the hand not being appropriated by Cait. "See? She got something we haven't seen before, too." His face turned up in a smug look. A small grin graced Cait's face, before disappearing.

Taylor grumbled. "Never mattered to you before." His hold tightened on Dinah. She glanced up at his face. He glared at Cait before lowering his gaze. Dinah needed to get Taylor alone and find out what was going on.

Cait watched, not adding anything. But a gleam lit up her eyes, watching the two men. "Why don't we all head for the mystery section? We can talk a little longer. Spend a little more time together."

Ian glanced at Dinah, then Taylor. "Sounds good. We aren't holding you up from anywhere, are we, Cait?"

"Oh, no. Not at all. Not any*one*, either." She batted her lashes at Ian, holding onto his arm. "Lead the way."

In the suspense section, Taylor scanned the shelves, walking back and forth along them.

"Here, let me hold the movies you've picked out." Cait finally released Ian's arm. "You two can help him look." Holding out a hand, she motioned. Ian handed over his box and Dinah did the same. They walked up and down the aisle looking at the suspense movies. Cait shadowed Ian, keeping in back of him.

So Dinah sidled up behind Taylor when the two of them were at the opposite side and slid in next to him. "Who is Cait?" she whispered, glancing quickly over to make sure Ian and Cait were still out of earshot.

"Ian's old girlfriend." Taylor's terse voice told her a lot of what she wanted to know.

"You two..."

"What?"

She leaned as close to him as she could get. "Was she in your relationship? As a threesome?"

Taylor's bark of a laugh shot from his throat like the rapid fire of a gun. "Hell, no."

Cait and Ian shot looks Taylor's way, who picked up a videotape, showing it to Dinah. Dinah pretended to giggle so they'd think that was the cause of his outburst. "What's up between you two?"

"All kinds of shit. She's a bitch. She doesn't want a threesome." Taylor's eyes glittered hard in the light. "She wants Ian, which Ian refuses to see. He's blind where she's concerned."

Cait and Ian approached too near for Dinah and Taylor to do any more talking. But Cait kept staring at her; she'd feel it and look over to find the woman's eyes boring holes in her. Cait's golden eyes registered her dislike of anything but Ian. But she never did anything blatant to show it so Ian would notice.

Taylor found a movie. "Found it. Where are Ian and Dinah's movies?"

"Oh." Cait's mouth pursed into a frown. "I was holding onto Ian so much, I put them down somewhere." Taylor looked pensive. They located the movies a few feet away, lying on a shelf.

After Cait finally let Ian go get in the car, Dinah watched her watch them from the back seat until the vehicle disappeared out of sight.

She turned back to find Taylor staring out of his window. Ian's hands were tight on the steering wheel. And neither spoke.

She folded her arms across herself, leaning back in her comfortable gray cushioned seat. Ian's car was much more comfortable than Taylor's red pickup truck. Ian's car was all gray, a luxury sedan. Not that he ever called it that. And he was quick to point out how fast the car could go.

When Taylor broke the silence a few minutes later, she'd been so lost in her own thoughts, she startled.

"So what's up with Cait?"

Ian didn't turn his head away from the road. "Nothing's up with Cait. We ran into her."

"Hrm. You know you never run into her. We've been going to that video store forever."

"Are you insinuating Cait was there to see us?"

"I'm more than insinuating it."

Dinah's head swiveled back and forth as she followed the conversation. Her stomach rolled up into a little ball down low in her abdomen.

"Now, Taylor…" Ian began, taking his hand off the wheel to put it in his lap. She frowned. They'd often hold hands. But Ian's irritation must have been keeping him from paying their usual attention to each other.

"Don't you 'Now, Taylor' me. I know you like her. You two were hot once. But the key is 'once.' You and Cait broke up for a reason."

"I don't understand why you don't like her." Ian's voice deepened with concern. "Why does she threaten you?"

"Oh, I'm not threatened. Not at all." Taylor's look said so much as his head turned to look at Ian. His face displayed his amusement. "I think she's threatened by me."

Ian made a sound, half a laugh and half a sigh. "That's rich, Taylor." He flipped back his sun visor. The setting sun created a vivid red canvas across the sky. Dinah surveyed it, turning in her seat, clearing her throat, not something she'd meant to do. She didn't mean to intrude upon the words they were having. Quickly, she glanced back up front.

Ian's eyes met hers in the rearview mirror for a split second, and Taylor glanced around at her. "Why don't we continue this later?" Taylor smiled at her.

"Sure."

Arriving home, Ian and Dinah put their keys on a shelf in the kitchen.

"You two, I swear. Peas in a pod." Taylor smiled at them.

"If you'd put your keys there..." Ian didn't finish as Taylor shot him the bird. "That's for later, isn't it?" Ian grinned, pulling her in for a tight hug. Taylor joined them.

She smiled, leaning into Ian's lean warmth as Taylor snuggled in closer to the side of them. This was more normal. "Are we going to watch a movie or what?"

Ian released them, heading for the small pantry beside the refrigerator. "I'll get the popcorn." His bare feet pattered on the tile.

Taylor moved to the fridge, opening it. "I'll get you and me drinks. Di, why don't we watch your movie first?"

Her smile grew. "Sure." She sometimes fell asleep after the first movie. They usually let her watch hers first because she was the most likely to get spooked. And his movie and Taylor's were both intense, from what she'd heard about them.

She popped the DVD in, barely looking at the case or disc. Grabbing the remote, she started to fast-forward – they usually had a ton of previews – but it started playing. She cocked her head to the side, watching, as the main menu emerged, not of her movie at all, but one of *Sleeping with the Enemy.*

Her heart pounding, she grabbed the remote, shutting the TV off. She'd seen the movie ages ago with Brad, hating every minute of it. It had given her nightmares. Brad's comments had filled her with horror.

"What a bitch," he'd railed near the end.

She'd looked at him aghast. "What?"

"That woman. Running from her man. Only time she should be done with her man is when he's done with her."

Lucky thing Brad was done with her. He had to be, he'd left her and hadn't tried to contact her since the beating.

Her eyes closed. That should have been a clue about Brad. So many things should have made her get out before he'd hurt her.

She panted, holding onto the DVD remote as if it were a lifeline. Her thoughts bandied back and forth like a tennis match. Why this movie? She'd almost stopped thinking of Brad daily.

"...ripped...Dinah, what's wrong?" She opened her eyes as Taylor looked at her sitting still on the couch. He rushed around the coffee table she had yet to move for their movie night. "What's up? Why haven't you started the movie?"

"It's...it's not the movie I picked." She stumbled over the words even as she said them.

Ian sat down on the other side of her, his weight tipping down the cushion. "What do you mean?"

"I mean it's not the movie I picked." She repeated it, the words doing less shaking. How has this happened? She'd picked up the case for *Bedazzled,* she was sure of it. "It's *Sleeping with the Enemy.*"

Taylor grabbed the case, turning it over in his hands. "But it says *Bedazzled* on this."

She leaned back further into the pillows. "I know that. But that wasn't what was inside. The DVD is different."

Taylor walked to the player and pressed eject. It shot out the slot that the DVD disk sat on. "It's *Sleeping with the Enemy.*" He held it up for Ian to view the title that she hadn't noticed when putting it in. "How did that get there?"

Ian rubbed a hand on her shoulders. "It probably got stuck back in the wrong case."

She nodded, trying to scoot in closer to him. "Probably." That had to be the explanation.

After putting the movie in the case and putting it on the coffee table, Taylor sat back down, his palms sliding up and down her legs. "Yeah. Sorry you didn't get your movie, though."

She blew out a long breath. "That's O.K. We can watch yours."

Ian laced a hand through hers. "You don't want to watch the one you ended up with, I take it?" He motioned to where the DVD case lay.

"No." She swallowed, a harsh sound. "I don't. I hated it when I saw it…before." Her hesitation told them who she'd seen it with. She quickly repeated, "But we can watch yours."

Taylor's hand came close to her inner thigh. It clenched under his roving attention. And most horribly, it brought home how close his hand was to her sex. Her womanhood. There were other names. It throbbed, making her want to press it into his palm. Her heart pounded again, with a different emotion than panic and anger pulsing through her veins. Taylor looked over the top of her head at Ian. "We don't have to watch ours tonight."

"We sure don't," Ian drawled, leaning down. His fingers stroked along her other side, mimicking Taylor's. "There are other things we could do for fun."

Her mouth dried out completely, the words creaking out between her lips. "Other things?"

Taylor traced her knee through her jeans, his touch feather light and sending tickles through the denim. "Other things."

Swallowing, she focused her attention on a painting of flowers on the wall. "I don't know, guys."

Taylor leaned forward to kiss her on the forehead, then stroked even further up her thigh. His touch made a shiver that went all the way down to her toes. How could he be so safe and sexy at the same time?

One finger pushed into her zipper, sliding down it. Once all the way down, it went slowly back up, stopping at the place where her bundles of nerves rested.

She squirmed in her seat.

Ian pushed her hair out of the way, his hands warm against her skin. His mouth bit softly on the side of her neck.

Another shiver rocked her.

Ian rolled his head up to lick at her earlobe. "If you feel uncomfortable, tell us. Enjoy yourself." He nibbled her neck ruthlessly, leaving no area on that side unattended.

She gasped, catching her breath. Her clothes weren't even off yet, and her heart pounded so hard she could barely hear anything else.

Taylor's hand slid away from her thighs and drifted up under her shirt. "Are you enjoying, Dinah?"

"Yessss." God help her but she was.

"Your nipples are so hard. So long." He pinched them through her bra, then moved it aside to do her bare skin.

And Brad's face flashed across her mind. He'd call her a slut. A whore. So would her family. No one had ever understood her relationship with Taylor. This would make it worse.

Taylor's hand stilled on her breast. She'd stiffened without realizing it. Ian leaned up to kiss her cheek. "Too much too soon?"

She closed her eyes, sinking further into the soft cushions. "Maybe."

They both withdrew slowly from her. And she felt the loss of them as if it were a kick in the gut. "I'm so sorry."

Taylor shook his head, his hair flowing with the motion. "It's O.K. I shouldn't have pushed it. I thought it might take your mind off things, but probably after everything tonight it was too much."

Ian's head swiveled and he stared quizzically at Taylor. "Yeah." His voice roughened with irritation.

Taylor moved to get up, and she placed a hand on his thigh. "Please don't move all the way away."

He stopped, taking her hand in his. "I won't, darling."

Ian stepped around the coffee table and pulled it back against the unused fireplace. "Let's get the movies going." He took one out of the case and started it. Stalking over, he positioned himself on the floor by Dinah, who still sat on the couch.

He grabbed her leg and yanked.

"Hey!" She yelped, almost falling right off the couch in surprise.

"Come on down here with me. Leave the Neanderthal alone."

She slid off the couch, laughing the whole time, to be beside Ian.

"Hey now." Taylor lowered himself onto the floor. "Pick on me, and I won't share the pillows." He pulled up the huge gray body pillow that stayed in the living room.

"Ahh. But I come equipped." Ian waggled his brows. "Well equipped." He pulled down the one from upstairs off the chair. "In more ways than one."

What a pair of nuts. And she loved them both and as more than friends. Startling to realize that. But she did. If only she could get past her inhibitions, she'd find her joy with them. But the question was, would she ever get past all that?

Chapter Five

Dinah drifted slowly awake, stretching onto her side. A body pillow lay against her. One eye peeked enough to see she was still in the living room. She let out a soft breath. Usually the guys carried her to bed.

She heard low voices. Her eye peeked again. In the darkness, lit only by low light streaming in from the windows, she could make out their profiles. They sat on the love seat. Letting the eye close, she lay still again, straining to hear.

The pillow rested right by her nose. Taylor's woodsy scent radiated from it. She buried her nose a little more in it to sniff.

Rustling sounded from the loveseat. She stilled her body. The cottony fabric tickled her nostrils. *No sneezing.*

"She's back settled. Let's try and keep our voices down so we don't wake her up," Ian said.

"I wasn't being loud."

Ian snorted lightly. "Now how do you figure that? What you told me."

"Because I'm in your life, and I don't mind sharing you. Unlike her."

They must be talking about Cait. Dinah swallowed. She didn't want to see them arguing. Not that she could see them, but she could hear it. It chilled her. She pulled the blanket further up, shuddering a little. Their positions didn't audibly change, and they kept talking. They must not have noticed her moving.

"Neither does she. Mind sharing me, that is."

"Since fucking when?"

"The last time she and I talked, she told me that."

"When did you two talk last?"

"I ran into her a week or so ago for the first time since forever. She wanted another chance as our third. I told her about Dinah."

"Ian." Taylor blew out a heavy breath. "Don't you think it's odd she'd turn up now? Now that we have Dinah in our lives more than we did."

"No, lover, I don't. I think it's coincidence. I don't understand your feelings toward her."

"Last time she was around, we almost broke up."

"She regrets all that. Says she's grown. And doesn't have a problem with a threesome anymore."

Another rustle. "You are so naïve it's not funny."

"Like you're worldly?"

Taylor let loose a snicker. She'd expected anger. Not amusement.

"Bite me."

"Gladly."

Both of them chuckled. And Taylor groaned.

Dinah opened her eyes enough to see that Ian had taken up the offer he'd himself made. Ian looked attached to Taylor's neck. And it looked as if his hand was in Taylor's lap. She could almost imagine Ian's smooth hand on the bulge.

"We are…" Taylor's breath hitched. "…trying things still with Dinah. Right?"

"Oh yeah. I don't intend to give up." Ian sounded winded. She couldn't see him, but wondered what Taylor was giving back to him. She'd bet it was a hand job through his pants as Ian was doing to him if Ian could reach him. The speculation about what they were doing to each other made her heart pound.

"Good."

"Bedroom?" She heard the rustle of them getting off the furniture.

"She probably won't wake up for a while. We'll bring her to bed…after…"

Soft footsteps plodded across the floor. She heard the slide of a door being shut.

And she was alone.

She'd never felt it more than at that moment.

Pushing up to sitting, she stared behind them. Twenty steps. That's all it was to the bedroom. Could she join them? They'd welcome her.

She rubbed a hand over her face, cursing herself. She hadn't been able to let them kiss and touch her earlier, much less go further. And why? Because she couldn't imagine herself in a ménage. It wasn't lack of desire or even attraction to both guys. She had that in spades. What was her problem?

"You're an idiot." The words made her sink down lower with the impact of their truth. Why did she care so much about what people thought? Especially Brad? Or her father?

Lying back down, she pulled both pillows up against her. Now she had both men's scents, the most comforting thing in the world she knew right now. And she drifted off to restless sleep.

* * *

On Monday, after a weekend of play, flirting and fun, Dinah sashayed into work.

"You look happy," Karen commented as she passed by.

"Do I?" Dinah smiled. Other than Friday night, it had been a nice weekend.

"Doesn't she?" A familiar voice passed by Karen in the hall. Cait stopped to lean against the entranceway as Dinah dumped her things onto her desk, then turning to face Cait. "Hi, Dinah."

"Hello, Cait. What are you doing here?" Dinah shook her head, hair flying as puzzlement filled her. What was Cait doing here? And looking unruffled and gorgeous. A man walking by checked out Cait's legs, which were barely covered by a pale pink miniskirt that matched her tight shirt. The woman knew how to get men's attention. Another man almost ran into the wall.

"I work here. A few doors down. You and the boys must have had a good weekend." Cait twirled her hair with her manicured fingertips.

"We did." Dinah resisted the urge to smooth down her own long skirt. She felt like a peasant in front of this woman. Again.

Cait stepped about three steps into her cubicle to say not so quietly, "Still holding out on them?"

Dinah's throat clenched so the words got trapped midlevel. It took a minute to get her voice back. "What?"

"Ian told me that you were reluctant to do it with those two." Cait grimaced. "Which I can't imagine. Or least not with Ian."

"My sex life is none of your business. And it's perfectly fine." The nerve of this woman. Dinah's shoulder's straightened.

"Let me give you some advice. Ian is a very sexual creature. If he doesn't get it, he's not happy." Cait tossed her hair back, looking smug. "Not that he ever was unhappy with me."

"He, Taylor, and I are very happy. Thank you so much for asking."

"Good. Because…well, I know how to push Ian's buttons, and when he's not satisfied, he always comes back to me. Ask Taylor." She flounced out of the opening. "Ciao."

Dinah pushed her hair back. What had happened with Cait? Had Ian gone to her and had sex? Without involving Taylor? She knew Taylor didn't mind Ian's sexuality with others as long as he knew beforehand or was involved in some way.

She still had the run-in with Cait on her mind as she walked to her car. The wind blew a warm breeze, tickling her skin. An old magnolia tree rested on the corner. Last summer, the blooms had been a treat walking into work. She rounded the corner, looking at the small dark green leaves. Her head came up suddenly, and she stared at what her brain had trouble processing.

Her car had been vandalized.

There were many dents, maybe from a hammer. And all over the hood and doors, "Whore" and "Slut" had been written.

"Oh, my god." Her eyes darted around, checking out the darkening street. Whoever did this could still be around. Clasping her pocketbook tighter, she turned to run and almost mowed down Karen.

"What's wrong, Dinah?" She moved her head to see around Dinah's body. "Ohhhhh. Looks like someone has it in for you."

Dinah's heart palpitated. "Would you walk me back into the building?"

"Sure. You better call security."

Once she was safe inside her building with more people, she intended to do that. And then, she'd call Taylor, waiting until he came before falling apart in his arms.

* * *

Taylor sprinted into the building.

Dinah stood in the lobby by a window, talking to a policeman while a security guard looked on. Pale and shaky on her feet, her voice came strong, the first thing he heard when he walked over.

"I parked there this morning. I have no idea why anyone would do this."

She saw him and pasted a wavery smile on her face.

He walked up and put one arm around her. The policeman eyed him. "I'm her friend. She called me for support and a ride." He met the older man's eyes without looking away. No way was he backing off from Dinah. This was the last thing she needed.

They finished up Dinah's statement, hopped in his truck, and headed home. But as he turned the corner and was stopped by a light, he saw her knuckles whiten. Her car was being loaded up onto a truck. It looked as if it had been pockmarked. Bright orange fluorescent curse words had been painted in huge swerving letters.

He reached his right hand from the steering wheel and put it on her knee. "I'm sorry. It will be O.K."

"Who could have done this?"

"I don't know, darling. I wish I did."

Her leg shook up and down. Her jaw pressed outward and was tight. He realized in addition to her fear, she was angry. That was a good sign. When she'd called, he'd worried about her state of mind. But he'd never seen her stronger than she'd acted with the police officer. "Brad...Brad hasn't been back around. He walked away. It couldn't have been him."

He didn't agree or disagree. Best she didn't know. He and Ian had made a conscious decision when Brad had showed up a couple of weeks ago, and then, begun calling, to keep her from finding out. Ian hoped they would wind up having to beat him up after what he'd done to Dinah. Dammit, if Brad had done this, he'd crossed the line from horrid ex to stalker.

She took a deep breath. "I hate this feeling. I've been feeling off balance since that stupid cockroach."

He tried to look over at her without ramming the car in front of him. "Huh? What cockroach?" She had cockroach issues. He'd seen her completely lose it over one in college. She'd been standing on a table while the little thing crawled around on the floor. And she hadn't slept at her apartment until it had been fumigated.

"The one that popped out of my lunch."

"It was in your lunch? Yuck."

"Tell me about it." A shudder racked her frame.

Something was going on. First the roach, then the movie. Now her car. Dammit, he should be able to protect her better than this. "You're sure you haven't seen Brad? Since he left?" Didn't think she had, but he had to be sure.

"No. No, I haven't." She put her hand over his. "I wouldn't want to, either."

"Good."

"I did run into Cait today."

"What?" He glanced at her again, this time taking his eyes off the road. When he glanced back, he had to slam on the brakes to avoid the car in front of him stopped at a light. "Cait came by to see you?" The bitch. She'd gotten her hooks into him once when Ian hadn't been listening. He wouldn't allow that to happen to Dinah.

"She's now working a few offices down from me."

Cait worked where Dinah did? Something didn't feel right. And it hit him, his hand banging the steering wheel. "Shit."

"What's wrong?"

"Nothing."

"Tell me."

"It's nothing."

She lightly smacked the hand still on her leg. "Tell."

"I think I know who did this to your car." And he was going to have some strong words with Ian's little stalker. Why the man couldn't see trouble with her, he didn't know. Last time, Ian had slept with her without him. And she'd gloated about it quite crowingly. They had almost broken up. Ian had promised to never do anything sexually without checking in. Which was all Taylor had asked for to start with. Damn woman. She was not going to endanger what they were close to having.

"Cait? Surely you don't think she did it?"

"I sure as hell do. She's a royal bitch."

"That doesn't mean she vandalized my car." Dinah didn't sound convinced, though. Shades of doubt inundated her tone.

He had no doubts. "Sure makes her a prime suspect."

"Taylor. It's O.K. You know, this may not have been singling me out. It might have been random. Let's go home and not think about it." She rubbed the back of her neck.

She had a point. The three events all sounded as if they were random occurrences. "I'll give you a massage when we get home."

"That would be lovely. Ian gave me one recently." Her smile was big as he glanced at her out of the corner of his eye.

"He told me. He enjoyed giving it to you." His choice of words caused some images to flash across his mind. Dinah and Ian making love in front of him. Now that would be a jerk-off dream. He shifted in his seat, his hard-on rising up plainly under his working khakis.

Pulling in, Taylor noticed that Ian's car was already home.

He ushered Dinah in to find Ian stewing, after having obviously showered and thrown on tight sweatpants with no shirt. "What the hell happened?" Ian snapped. "Why didn't you call me back?" His wet hair hadn't seen a comb and went off in every direction.

Dinah's eyes widened in surprise, but even she couldn't disguise a flash. She'd been looking at Ian's abs and hips with lust in her eyes. Her cheeks pinkened with a beguiling flush.

Oh, darling. Nothing turned Taylor on more than to see her passion coming out. She wanted them. She couldn't hide it. But she'd come from a rigid family who viewed anything different as bad. It had been hard for her in college to even do any normal sexual experimenting. He remembered all the times she'd guiltily confided in him, expecting some sort of recrimination. Ménages weren't the norm. Even he had taken a while to digest having one.

Both of them stared at him. He shifted on his feet. Oh yeah, he'd been asked a question. "You must have been in the shower when I left you the message."

"That much I know, dammit. What happened to her car? Why did you have to go get Dinah?"

Dinah spoke up before he could, surprising him by volunteering to be the leader in talking about it. "My car was vandalized. Someone hit it with what looked like a hammer and spray-painted it."

Ian's eyes lifted to Taylor's with surprise, then anger. He rubbed the back of his neck.

Taylor nodded. "It was pretty bad."

"Shit."

Dinah shrugged. "It's probably a random act."

"Probably." Ian glowered and then cast a glance his way. Ian was thinking Brad. Taylor had had that thought, but Cait seemed a much more viable candidate. Time to put that theory out there.

"Cait's working at Dinah's workplace."

"What?" Ian's face contorted with honest shock. "She is?"

"Yeah." Ian hadn't known. Another mark in the plus column for Cait.

His eyes met Taylor's. "She hadn't told me that."

"I figured."

Dinah waved a hand, bringing their attention back to her. "It was probably someone random. I don't want to discuss it anymore. I want to eat."

Smiling, Taylor said, "Yes, ma'am." She rarely stood up to make a decision on what they should do.

He followed her into the kitchen, watching the gentle sway of her ass and hips. Damn, what a nice ass she had. He couldn't help a gentle pat, which made her jump.

Ian laughed softly from behind them. "Isn't he grabby?"

Though she blushed, her eyes sparkled. "Yeah, he sure is."

"Hey, now." After putting water on to boil, Taylor pulled out some spaghetti for them. "Oh, you should have seen Dinah talking to the cop, though. Calm. Cool." He focused his attention on her. "You did a great job, darling."

"Thank you." She pulled her hair back behind her ear. "I was nervous."

When she'd been with Brad, he'd handled everything. Same thing had happened with her family. Taylor had been proud of how she'd reacted to the situation, taking over the responsibility herself. "You didn't show it at all."

He poured the pasta into the pan.

Ian reached over and lifted Dinah onto the counter by the sink. A couple of canisters scooted to the back, clanking behind her.

"What was that for?"

"Maybe you look good enough to eat." Ian pushed in with his body between her knees. He purred, canting his head up along her middle.

"Ian."

"You do."

Taylor stirred the pasta, watching.

Ian dropped to his knees on the tile floor. Dinah peered over to see where he went. "What are you doing? Bowing?"

"Are you my queen? Should I bow?"

"Why, yes, I think you should." She drew herself up, sticking out her neck regally. Her playful side was coming out. This was going to be quite a show.

With a wink at Taylor, Ian bowed down. Shifting up further on his knees, he took her small foot in his hands.

"What are you doing now?"

Pushing his thumbs into her arch, he massaged. "I'm going to kiss and massage the feet of my Queen, of course."

Taylor continued to fix the food, sneaking peeks at his friend and his lover. Dinah's gulp had him glancing their way. Ian had sucked her toe into his mouth and was obviously using one very talented tongue to his advantage.

Taylor hardened more. Dinah had flushed again, reclining back on the counter. Her tongue swiped out to lick her lips.

He lost it. Any control he had went into limbo. Stalking over, he placed one hand at the base of her neck and dove in to kiss her. Her arm wrapped around his neck. His kiss wouldn't be gentle nor would it end. Their mouths and tongues playfully danced and darted in the most sensual wet way.

It was Ian's movements when he released her foot and jumped to his feet that brought their kiss to an end. Ian grabbed the pot off the stove. All the water had burned up and the spaghetti was starting to. Turning down the heat, he poured a little water into the pan.

"Shit." Taylor rubbed his chin. "Sorry about that."

Ian's grin ate up his face. "You were distracted."

Dinah's head ducked down. She didn't say a word.

Taylor clasped her hand tightly in his. "Damn right, I was. And loving the distraction, too."

"I'm sorry," she whispered.

"Darling, don't be. But I'd suggest we do takeout. And don't touch each other for awhile if you're starving for food." She licked her lips again. Taylor groaned. "Or do that." She blinked at him, puzzled.

"Taylor has a thing for tongues." Ian grabbed the phone. "Chinese O.K. with everyone? They deliver and are quick."

"Sure." Taylor tried to remember all the philosophers he enjoyed reading. How he would get through this meal without jumping anyone after what had happened, he didn't know. His cock twitched. It wasn't going to be easy.

"We can do strawberries and chocolate for dessert." Good thing Ian stood out of reach or Taylor would have smacked him. Nothing beat strawberries and chocolate while using a lover for a plate.

"You know, I'm not all that hungry." Dinah's voice came out tiny in the room, but it echoed in his ears. There was no way to interpret that any other way than how he did. Especially with her throaty voice reflecting her desire from minutes ago.

"You're not? Are you sure?"

Ian's hand stood poised to dial. "You're not hungry? For food?"

She shook her head. "I'm not. Though the strawberries and chocolate sound good."

"They sound good?" Ian laid the phone down and bolted to the fridge. He and Ian were reacting exactly alike. They both were on alert. They knew Dinah wanted this but was unsure of herself. This was the first instance she'd initiated. They damn sure weren't going to miss it.

"Oh, yeah."

Taylor slung Dinah over his shoulder.

"What are on earth are you doing?" She laughed, her head at the top of his back.

"Carrying you to bed, my Queen. To worship you as I should." He continued the game she and Ian had been playing.

The short walk down the hall was all it took for Dinah's desire to ebb. He felt it in the stiffening of her body. She bit her lip as he tossed her in the middle of the huge bed.

"Don't." He slid down on the bed by her, rubbing her arm. "Trust us."

"I do. But this…I don't know."

The fact that the words that were her greatest fears had been painted on her car wasn't lost on him. Whether it was Cait or Brad, someone was going to pay. "It doesn't make you bad. Or a slut or whore that you want us. It's different. But it's what you're feeling. Let us show you what it can be."

Chapter Six

Dinah rubbed where Taylor had. In the kitchen, she'd been so hot when Ian had been kissing her and Taylor's eyes had lit up. He'd stalked over to her as if he couldn't resist her and started kissing her, too. She'd felt desirable. Hard not to when a man's eyes burned a hole through you. She'd felt loved. That was one thing that made them so sexy to her.

But walking down the hall, all the old voices had started up. Nothing she'd ever been raised with had prepared her for this.

Ian sauntered in with berries, chocolate and some whipped cream.

Somehow from the way Taylor had reacted to Ian's comment, she didn't think they'd be snacking.

"Darling, we're going to take this slow. Any time you don't like what we're doing, we stop."

Ian nodded, reaching around to pull Taylor's t-shirt over his head. "What he said."

Two hard bodies stood next to the bed. Washboard abs. Taylor's body was golden with small, crisp hairs. Ian was paler and had darker hair.

And two clearly visible outlines of erections strained against sweatpants and khakis. Obviously, this was turning them on as much as it was her. Between her thighs felt slippery. They were too damn sexy.

When her eyes climbed back up, they both looked rather smug.

Pure mischief flared in her. "Get over yourselves. Any woman would look down there."

Taylor laughed out loud as he scrambled over the bed to the other side of her.

Ian grasped a strawberry with lean fingers, sitting on the bed by her. He held it out. "Here you go." She reached to take it. "Noooo. Take it with your mouth, honey."

"Are you feeding me this?" Ian had said that when she came into their relationship, they would feed her. She wasn't sure she was taking on this spot permanently, and wasn't willing to do anything to make them think she was.

"Nah. This is a snack."

Dinah took a small nibble from the berry. It tasted sweet and dribbled cool juice. She licked a speck off her bottom lip.

Taylor reached out to gently stroke where the spot had been. "Let me make sure that's clean for you." He dipped down to kiss her. The kiss was startling in its gentleness.

Ian's eyes were bright as he offered another strawberry, this one dipped in chocolate. She nipped off the part covered in the sweet.

After she'd chewed, Taylor dipped in again. This time, he picked up a berry and fed it to her.

"Aren't you two going to eat?" She mushed the berry up inside her mouth after asking. Her tongue tumbled out to catch liquid on her lips. And she liked the way Taylor's eyes followed it.

Ian lowered his hand to the plate of offerings, waving beside it. "You want to feed us? Go right ahead."

As a matter of fact, she did. She grabbed a huge berry, dipped it in chocolate and lifted it to Taylor.

His bite was precision, taking off the very bottom of the fruit, then sucking it into his mouth and grinding it. Oh my. She'd never imagined watching someone eat a strawberry could be so sexy.

"I have chocolate on my mouth." He pointed to a nonexistent speck at the corner.

Ian swooped to kiss and lick, taking care of the invisible drip.

Dinah's stomach bottomed out at the sight of the two men kissing. Her thighs clenched with the force of an arousal she'd never experienced so strongly.

When the kiss finished, Ian turned toward her with a sated look. With shaking hands, she proffered the new chocolate-covered fruit. He didn't take the berry into his mouth at first, but lapped off the chocolate, his tongue circling round and round the bottom of the berry. It wiggled the tip back and forth.

Dinah's breathing raced along with her heartbeat. Her sex moistened while her mouth dried.

Taylor grunted as the berry disappeared into Ian's mouth, shifting on the bed. "I have got to get out of these pants."

"Go for it." Ian leaned back on a pillow as if to get a better view.

Taylor's gaze shot to Dinah.

No way could she form a coherent sentence, so she nodded. What was she doing? Here with two men? But walking away wasn't a good option. She'd tried that, and had regretted it.

Taylor undid the top button and slid down the zipper. He shrugged the khakis off his slim hips. His erection sprang free with a jerk.

She didn't even notice the pants going down the rest of the way. Her eyes wouldn't pull away from Taylor's cock. Long and rouged with arousal, it perked up under her scrutiny.

When she finally looked away from Taylor settling on the bed again beside her, Ian's eyes were studying her. "God, you're sexy." He brushed her hair back from her face

She flushed more than she had already. She still wore her long skirt and light sweater. Not exactly seduction attire.

Ian grabbed a berry and held it out to her. She leaned forward to take it with her mouth and Ian pulled it out of reach.

"Huh?"

Very slowly, deliberately, he leaned over and placed the berry above Taylor's member, at the base of it.

Taylor let loose a gasp. "That's chilly."

Ian maneuvered it until it didn't fall away. "Go get it. And not with your hands."

She swallowed, looking at them both. She'd have to go very close to Taylor's erection and move him out of the way. Could she do that?

"Go for it, darling. My cock don't bite." He leaned back, his hands pulling back. He wouldn't touch her while she did this.

Trying to keep her eyes on the berry was impossible. He sat right there. His cock, so he'd called it.

Slowly, she reached out with one hand, grasping him and moving him so she could get the berry. His hips shifted. "Oh, darling."

Her hold was loose. She tightened it, wrapping her fingers around. He jerked in her hand.

Moving his cock over, she leaned her head in to pick up the berry in her mouth.

One grunt from him at the brief touch of mouth on skin, and it was done. Her fingers skimmed up his length, toyed in the already moist tip, and released him.

"Damn it."

"Did I hurt you?" She looked at him, concerned.

"No." Taylor swiveled his hips. "Not at all."

"Too excited for this, lover?" Ian sounded winded.

"Almost."

Ian stood up. "My turn to strip."

Taylor's darkened eyes regarded him. "So get to it."

Ian's face sought Dinah's. "You O.K. with this?"

"Sure." She nodded. Taylor was already naked. What was one more naked man? She'd get to see Ian for the first time. Taylor had talked about him a lot when they'd first gotten together.

Ian's hands slid down to his hips, grasping the sweatpants material in limber fingers, sliding them down his narrow hips and legs. His cock sprang free with a slight jump. Ian's erection was thick and heavy, his cock reddened, with a glistening plum-shaped tip. Damn, he was huge.

She caught her lip between her teeth. Desire raced through her at seeing Ian's naked form. Her heart pounded even as she stiffened. She scooted back on the bed.

How did two men work with one woman sexually?

Not anything she'd thought about with her fear of being with them and then, her arousal tonight. She should have asked so many questions before now. She tried to remember what Taylor had told her, but drew a blank. He hadn't told her anything specific that came to mind. Did a man take a woman up...her butt while the other took her regularly? Surely not. Wasn't that reserved for men to do to each other? Ian and Taylor took each other that way, but she couldn't imagine one of them doing that to her. Of course, a few months ago, she couldn't imagine this going on.

"Dinah." Ian sat on the bed in front of her, his erection poking out like a slanted exclamation point. He tipped her head away from looking at his cock. "I won't hurt you."

"I know." Neither of them would do anything she didn't want or anything she told them not to. It gave her a certain freedom. She could call a stop to this whenever she wanted. And maybe she would. Soon.

"There are a few ways you can take both of us. I don't have to take you anally. I know you were thinking about that." She opened her mouth. Ian pressed fingers against it. "I know you. I'd like to show you how pleasurable I can make it this time." His lips slid in to nuzzle her neck. Taylor joined him, nuzzling the back of her as Ian continued, "But I won't push for that tonight."

Ian palmed her breast through the light sweater, circling her nipple with fingers until it hardened. She closed her eyes against the sensations. "You're wearing too many clothes. Isn't she, Taylor?" Dinah's eyes shot open wide.

"Oh, yeah."

She swallowed. Somehow with her clothes on, it had seemed as if she could still walk away. This would be crossing a line, a big one. And it meant getting naked in front of the two almost godlike men that graced this bed. Would they like her body? Curiosity of what their reactions would be made her bold.

They helped her to her feet and waited, two naked men sitting on a huge bed, both of them highly aroused over being with her. Unbelievable.

She undid the small button to her skirt, seeming to take twice as long as usual doing it. After unzipping it, she let the skirt fall to her ankles. Stepping out of it, she turned her attention to the sweater. She'd picked blue satin bikini briefs this morning. They were already soaked. God, could they tell how wet she was? Insults echoed in her mind, swirling with images of her car. But this felt so...right. How could it be wrong for her to be with men she loved?

Without thinking too much more, she pulled her sweater over her head to reveal the matching demi bra. She didn't want to think. She wanted their reaction to her nakedness. Hardly looking at them, shaking her head to get her hair in line, she reached around her back to unsnap her bra.

"Stop." Taylor's guttural voice stopped her. His breath moved harshly in his chest. "Come here."

"I thought you wanted my clothes off?"

"We do. But stop there. Dammmmn."

She took two steps to the bed, and they parted to let her slide in between them. Neither could keep their eyes away from her.

"She's every man's fantasy, isn't she?" Ian blew out a breath. "Pair of high-heeled shoes, and call me Rover, I'd beg."

Both sets of hands began a slow gentle assault on her senses. They touched the small strips of satin cloth that covered her. They touched the exposed skin. Taylor's hands were the rougher of the two. Ian's had smooth contours that tickled the sensitized nerves.

Taylor's hand ran along her inner thigh for several passes, sliding ever closer to flesh that needed to be touched, wanted to be touched. Dinah whimpered as his fingers slid under the flimsy material.

"Like that?"

"Uh huh." His big hand had trouble navigating the narrow way until she was about ready to pull the underwear off herself. "Take them off, please."

He bumped the back of his hand across the small expanse of material that covered her innermost self. "Take this off?"

"Yes." Was it possible to explode? Because it sure felt as if her head was about ready to pop.

His other hand stopped at the top, brushing against her pubic bone. "You sure?"

"Take it off!"

His warm chuckle at her outburst flushed her skin even more. Carefully, he slid the material down her legs, then his fingers dove in, one of them encircling the bundle of nerves that invited his touch.

"Ohhhh." She leaned further back, until Ian propped her up slightly.

"Time for this to come off, too." He undid the back catch to her bra and slid it down her arms. He slid back to the headboard, widened his legs, sliding her back along him. His erection rested against the small of her back, brushing it, bumping against it. She shivered at the feel. His hands centered on her breasts, touching and pulling.

When a breath floated across her pubic hair, she jumped, opening her eyes. Taylor had positioned himself right above her sex. Helplessly, she looked down at him. He planted a kiss at the top where her hair began. And he licked his way inside her first with a long swipe of tongue. Then he made little passes that had her writhing. Her hips swiveled, her whole body twisting.

One man was touching her breasts and wringing out her pleasure there. Another was tasting her as if she were a dessert worthy of kings. And all she could do was rock back and forth, lost in sensations.

Ian's voice sounded as if it came from far away. "Turn her over a little."

Taylor must have heard because he helped to ease her off of Ian, but his tongue and teeth never stopped their ministrations. She now lay on her side, with Taylor still between her thighs, one leg partially above his head. She'd never been so exposed to anyone before.

A squirting sound had her opening her eyes to try to find Ian. But Taylor was too involved in what he was doing and soon pulled her back to only focus on his mouth.

With a gentle swipe, Ian's finger skimmed her backside lightly and slid to her anus. Her butt cheeks clenched.

"Ian." Her voice was shaky. She was so close to coming. Taylor kept inching her closer, but not giving her total manipulation from his mouth. If she could get it, it would happen. But what was Ian doing?

"Shhhh. I'm playing, honey."

The finger rimmed her. She realized it was slippery. Lube. And then Taylor sucked her into his mouth. Her whole body straightened into a spasm.

And Ian's finger went slightly into her hole. She moaned at the feelings, both of being licked and of being breached like this. In and out, the finger slid.

The orgasm rocked her body with a crescendo that had her spiraling along waves of pleasure back to earth.

"Ohhhhh." Taylor didn't stop even as she lay weakly beside him, aftershocks rocking her. She was about to say she didn't think she could take any more, when another Ian finger rimmed her. Intense pressure built as they slid into her. Two fingers rested inside. "Ian…"

Cold moisture slid down onto her. More lube. The fingertips slickened. But the pressure built. "Give it a minute. It will ease."

Taylor tipped her clit with only the point of his tongue, putting more and more push on it.

The pressure in her backside did ease off slowly to a dullness.

Ian was preparing her to take him. To ram that huge cock up in her. There was no way. He wouldn't fit there.

She stiffened.

Ian added another finger, causing her to jump. "Don't fight it. Relax. "

"Relax, darling. Concentrate on my mouth."

It wasn't that hard to do. Taylor knew what she liked and used it to take her mind off of Ian's fingers.

She'd adjusted to Ian's fingers when the next orgasm sucked her into its wake, leaving her trembling and sweating. Taylor slowly withdrew himself from her, smacking his lips. He pulled on a condom. "You're going to feel so good." He rolled it up on himself with eager hands.

Ian's fingers left her.

What were they going to do exactly?

Taylor guided her down onto the bed on her back. "I'm taking you this time this way. Next time, Ian will." The words "next time" both warmed her and filled her with fear. Would there be a next time?

Ian tossed a wipe to the floor - he'd obviously wiped his hands. "Your choice, Dinah. I can take Taylor while he takes you. Or..."

"Or?" She shivered with the knowledge she was going all the way with this. No thinking now, too late to turn back. It might be her only time, but she was going to do this.

"You can take me in your mouth. It's your call."

They waited expectantly for an answer. Love surged through her. They were letting her decide so many things in this play. "My mouth."

Taylor leaned down to kiss her. "Good choice."

They situated themselves with Taylor above her, Ian to the side. When Taylor surged inside her, he groaned. "So tight."

"You should have felt her ass." Ian semi-kneeled so that she could reach his member. When she tapped it with her tongue, he startled. He tasted salty from the pre-come.

Taylor thrust quickly into her, then paused, seeking some control, before he moved more slowly. "Don't say that, man."

"Her ass was so tight. It's going to grip you like nothing ever has." Ian's head rolled back as she ran her tongue around the rim of his cock, laving the edges.

"Asshole," Taylor gasped.

"Damn straight." Ian's hand clenched as Dinah pulled him fully into her mouth, suctioning up and down his length.

"She needs to come again," Taylor pronounced.

Dinah's eyes widened. She couldn't disengage Ian to tell him she didn't think she could handle another climax. But then Taylor changed the pressure, changed the angle he thrust down into, deepening it. Her swollen sex clutched at him. One of his fingers pinged her clit. And Ian pressed his cock down deeper into her mouth.

And impossibly, a climax flared and went off like a rocket inside her head, with lights and colors swirling all around.

As her climax rocketed off, Ian's grunt and moan told her he was close. Taylor answered him with sounds of his own. They were both close. And both got hit at almost the same time. Ian's seed spurted into her mouth, filling it, as Taylor jerked, his whole body spasming, calling her name.

Taylor collapsed on top of her, limp and sweaty. "Ohhhhh."

Panting, Ian swatted his ass, and then grabbed the condom, tossing it into the trashcan. He rejoined them as they intertwined legs and arms into one big pile on the bed.

He kissed her, open-mouthed, on the lips. "Thank you. For trying this. You won't be sorry."

They both were asleep within minutes, both of them enfolding her in strong and different arms.

Dinah scrubbed her face with a hand she moved away from them. It had been the most glorious thing she'd ever been a part of. An expression of a commitment she didn't yet feel. They loved her and trusted her enough to bring her into their relationship. Was love enough? She loved them. But in the quiet of the bedroom, doubts ebbed their way back into her mind.

Chapter Seven

Ian slipped out of bed early, heading to the kitchen. Both Dinah and Taylor were curled up into little balls. Sort of like kittens. Only it hadn't been kittens and sweetness last night. His cock swung up to early morning readiness. But first he had something to do.

He dialed the phone, not caring how early it was.

"Hello?" A sleepy voice answered the phone.

"Hi, Cait."

"Iannn." Her voice purred. He heard the rustle of blankets in the background. "You're up early."

"Cait, why didn't you tell me you worked with Dinah?"

A pause. "I thought I had."

"No, I would have remembered that. Why, Cait?" Getting a job where Dinah worked must have been deliberate on her part.

She sighed. "I don't know."

"Did you do it?" Cait always had a plan. He had trouble believing that plan involved vandalism. But she'd kept a secret about where she worked.

"Do what?"

"Dinah's car."

"What about it?"

Her voice sounded honestly perplexed. "The vandalism."

"I didn't do anything to Dinah's car. I swear that." He heard more rustling. "She's not your type, Ian. I know you."

"You didn't think Taylor was my type either." Old territory to get into.

"He's not."

Ian closed his eyes, leaning against the door jamb. "He is."

"We were so happy together..." Her voice took on a plaintive note.

Dammit. He would be less angry if she hadn't played the hurt card. "You knew what I was when we got involved. I told you what it would be like. You couldn't handle it. Taylor can."

"That little twerp Dinah can't. I bet she hasn't even given it up for you. I would. You know that? I'd even do Taylor if that's what you wanted."

"That's not what I want. I want a woman who can be lovers with Taylor and me. Because that's what *she* wants." Cait had never been serious about a threesome. She wanted to do it because she thought that's what he would accept. He turned as a noise came from the bedroom. "And that is Dinah." It was. She hadn't accepted it yet. Society's and her family's morals hung heavy around her heart. But eventually, she'd find a way to yank them off with his and Taylor's help. Cait's issues ran much deeper than Dinah's. Maybe that was because they'd been together first, before anyone else. He'd never know, though. "You need to move on, Cait." He softly hung up the phone.

Taylor's voice spoke quietly behind him. "I know you keep hoping she'll become what you need. Because of your feelings for her. But she's not going to."

He turned to face Taylor. "I know."

Taylor wrapped arms around him for a big kiss. "She's a bitch, too."

"Taylor."

Taylor merely shrugged. "So she did do Dinah's car?"

"She denied it. Didn't seem to know anything about it. So I don't think so." She'd seemed genuine on that, at least to him.

Frowning, Taylor dropped his arms. "That only leaves one person."

"Brad."

And they didn't know where exactly he was, damn the asshole.

* * *

Later that day, getting back from grocery shopping, Dinah cackled over something that Ian said. He'd made her laugh all through the grocery store. "I'm going to check messages."

"Hey, let me." Taylor pushed ahead of her. "I'll check later. Let's get this shit put away right now"

She blinked at him, curiously. "I can hit play."

"You know how Taylor doesn't like putting away groceries. He wants to get it done." Ian pulled things out of a bag.

She'd seen the light blinking on the answering machine even as Taylor grasped her arm and pulled her away. "But there's a message."

"I'll get it in a minute."

Her eyes switched between them. "What's going on?" When had the last time she'd checked messages been? She couldn't remember. They usually did it. She wasn't sure why she'd offered this time, but why were they trying to keep her from the machine and the message?

"Nothing." Taylor tossed her bread. "Put this away."

She flung it into the bread box. "Something is going on. What is it? Who's been calling me?" The answer was obvious. Her heart froze, not beating through icy tendrils of fear wrapping itself about her whole middle. "Brad."

Ian shut the refrigerator door with a clank. "Dinah. It doesn't matter."

"It does. You two kept this from me." She couldn't believe they would do this, not after all their talks.

"We didn't want you hurt again." Taylor ran a hand across his face. "That's the last thing you need right now."

"You should have told me. I would have dealt with it." She stomped over to the answering machine. They'd had no right to keep this from her. Whether she wanted to talk to

Brad or not was her decision. Her finger smushed the play button.

Brad's voice filled the kitchen. "Dinah, you little whore. Call me. Tonight. Stop ignoring me."

Her hand clutched the counter tightly as the hateful voice scraped across her senses. Taylor stalked to her in an instant. "It's O.K." He pulled her into his strong arms. "Don't call him."

"I'm not going to." The desire to be with Brad didn't nick at her heart anymore. He'd given that up when he'd hit her, even if it had taken her a while to realize that. Each blow had driven her feelings in like nails too deep down. His loss still stung. But she didn't want to be with him anymore. She meant it when she said she wasn't calling him.

"Tell the asshole to take a flying leap." His hand rubbed up and down her back, the touch soothing.

Brad's calling hadn't been something she'd expected. He'd been done with her when he'd broken it off. Nor had she expected Ian and Taylor to keep this from her.

She pulled away from Taylor's touch. "You shouldn't have hidden this."

"We wanted to protect you."

"I don't need protecting."

Ian piped up, still standing in the kitchen. "We thought it was best not to tell you."

"You were wrong." She puffed out a breath. "I bet Brad did my car. I thought he wasn't around."

"We don't know where he is." Taylor tried to take her hand, and she pulled it away from him.

"If you see him, I want to be told what's going on. Don't keep things from me."

Ian nodded. "We can do that."

"You'd better." She stalked off, grabbing her purse. "I'm going out. I need to think." She had her hand on the door before Taylor spoke.

"You don't have a car. Take mine."

* * *

Coming back to the house, Dinah hesitated as she pulled up. Most of her anger had fled. But she still felt betrayed that they'd keep it from her.

Before she could get out, Brad stepped out of a car parked on the street.

Her heart raced as she looked to the house. No time to run. He'd be on her before she could make it. She could lock herself in the car and blow the horn. But that would give the man exactly what he wanted. Her cowering in fear. Instead, she stepped out of the car to face him. If he hit her, she could scream.

"You little filthy whore."

How many times had she heard those words from him? But the embarrassment and shame didn't come this time. "What do you want, Brad?"

"How dare you shack up with those fags?" He snarled the words, stepping even closer into her space. "I've been waiting to catch you alone."

She held her ground. "I asked what you wanted." How far she had come. A few months ago, she'd have been trying to placate him. Now all she could think about was how he'd hurt her.

"I want you back."

"No." It felt good to deny him. And he wasn't what she wanted for her life, she knew that now. She didn't want a man who hit her. Who tore her down with words. She'd had that enough from her father.

"How dare you play the whore for them? And tell me no." He raised his hand to backhand her. She didn't flinch. Brad's eyes widened in shock at her lack of reaction. His mouth widened to an O. But his hand stayed ready to strike her.

"Wouldn't do that."

Taylor and Ian had stepped out onto the front step. Both of them looked murderous and had their arms folded across their chests.

"Like you could stop me, fag boys."

Taylor took three steps, then shook his head. "You aren't worth it. But the boys in blue will stop you."

"You called the cops, you pansy ass."

"Damn right." Ian glowered. "Dinah, back away from him."

"I'm fine here. Brad was leaving. Weren't you, Brad?"

Brad shook a fist at the two men. "They've manipulated you. They've put you up to this."

"No, you did. When you hit me."

"I came to say I was sorry about two months after it happened. I called. Lots of times. You never returned my calls."

Brad had showed up to apologize? Dinah looked at Ian and Taylor, who looked at her guiltily. It didn't make a difference as to how she thought of Brad. Not anymore, though she couldn't be sure how it would have back then. But it colored her thoughts about her lovers. They hadn't exactly lied, but they hadn't told her the truth either. And there had been lots of calls. They'd kept so much from her under the guise of protecting her. Dammit. Damn them. All the talk about trusting her. "It doesn't matter." It didn't matter for her and Brad. But for her, Ian and Taylor it mattered a lot.

"They kept you from me. Bastards."

"Go home, Brad. It doesn't matter." He stood glaring at her. "And leave me alone from now on. My car and all."

"What about your car?"

"You vandalized it." Sirens sounded in the far distance. Taylor and Ian hadn't been bluffing. They had called the police.

"I haven't done anything to your car." He took two steps back, clenching his hands in by his side. "You'd choose these fucking fags over me?"

"Any day of the week."

At the same time, Ian snorted. "Like we believe you on her car."

Brad had looked surprised. Dinah thought he was telling the truth. Maybe it had been a random act and nothing directed specifically at her.

With a huff, Brad dashed for his car. "You can have them. Little whore."

* * *

After everything had settled down, Dinah looked at Ian and Taylor, who sat across from her at the kitchen table. "We need to talk." She prayed for strength to not hurt them, but to do what she knew she needed to do.

Taylor blew out a soft sigh. "We should have told you about Brad."

"Yeah. You should have. I don't blame you, though." Now that she'd had a little time to think about it. She rested her hands on the table. "I realized something tonight. Because of everything that's happened."

"What's that?" Ian put his arm across the back of Taylor's chair.

"I need to be on my own for a little while."

"Why?" Taylor's eyes had a hurt cast to them. Not her intent. She reached over and grasped his hand in hers.

"Because it would be too easy to let you two take care of me. That's what you did about my finances. And Brad. That's what I allowed Brad to do, before. It's what my father did even when I should have been on my own. I realized I have to take care of myself first before I can be with anyone."

"We aren't your father. Or Brad." Taylor swallowed.

"I know that." She squeezed his hand. "But if I'm going to be with you two, I need to stand on my own first. Something I haven't done yet. Otherwise, you two will end up doing what you did. Protecting me, and you might do it from everything." The two strong men would overwhelm her unless she was more sure of herself. Distance was the only thing that would give her faith in herself.

"Are you going to come back to us?" Taylor's eyes still looked pained, but there was a hopeful spark in them.

She pinched the bridge of her nose. "I don't know. I love you both. A lot. But I almost let my fears about what everyone else thought take over what I have with you. I need to figure out how I feel about our relationship without hearing my father calling me a whore in my mind." All her thoughts had been tainted. She didn't know how she felt about being with them both. And only being away from their strength would tell her.

"I love you." Taylor huffed out a breath.

"As do I." Ian reached over to put his hand on theirs. "Try not to take too long."

She half-smiled. "I won't."

"Where are you going to go? I bet we could find an apartment..." Ian broke off as she cocked her head at him. "I'm doing it again, aren't I?"

"Yes. Yes, you are. I'll find my own place." They both clasped her hand in theirs instead of it covering their hands.

"We'll help you move in." Taylor flexed a bicep, showing off a huge muscle. She'd miss those strong arms holding her at night. "We are the muscles."

She giggled. "Yes, you two are." She sobered, looking at the floor. "I don't know how long…"

Taylor squeezed her hand and so did Ian. "We know. Take all the time you need."

But they wouldn't wait for her.

It saddened her. But she couldn't allow them to eat her alive, and they would if she went into a relationship with them right now. If only she'd find her center before they found a third.

Chapter Eight

Dinah sighed, carrying a dish of macaroni and cheese. Taking a deep breath, she knocked on the door. Her parents had invited her over for Sunday dinner. She wasn't sure of the reception she would get. Well, she knew her father would find fault with everything. He always did. But it was the first time she'd been over to their house since she and Brad had broken up. At first, it had been their choice. Then it had become hers. Her mother had begged her to come back, and she'd finally felt strong enough to do it.

She'd been on her own for almost eight months, living by herself, taking a new job, and getting some counseling. Taylor and Ian had come to see her many times on her lunch break, but she hadn't hung out with them much beyond that, even as friends. God, she missed them. Times like this she wanted to run into their comforting arms.

Her mother opened the door. "Hi, Dinah!" She grabbed her in a hug. "I'm glad you could make it today."

"Don't be hugging the girl outside like that. What will the neighbors think?" Her father's low baritone came from the easy chair in the living room. Exactly where he had always been. Football echoed from the TV that sat a few feet away.

Her mother ducked her head, quickly ushering in Dinah, cowering and doing what her father said, as always.

Brad smirked at her from the couch nearby her dad. "Hello, Dinah."

"Hi, Brad. What are you doing here?" Other than irritation, she didn't feel anything when she looked at him, despite her surprise at seeing him in her parents' home. She straightened up her shoulders with a smile.

Her mother bounced nervously on her feet, head bobbing up and down, too. "He's going to have lunch with us." Her mother always acted so anxious. Had she been on her way to being like that? Damn, she had. Cowering, unable to make a simple decision without worrying about it being right. She sucked in a deep breath.

"Yeah, maybe you'll come to your senses. And quit being a whore to those fags."

Dinah's mouth clenched. Anger hung low in her belly. It was the first time her father's insults had elicited a response. Or at least, one she'd acknowledged. One last look at her mother determined it. She wasn't going to wind up living in fear like that.

"I'm not a whore." She met her mother's troubled eyes and shoved the macaroni to her. Stalking over, she planted herself in front of her father, blocking his TV. "I'm not a whore, Dad."

"Dinah, your dad is watching football." Her mother stood there, wringing her hands together.

"What do you call shacking up with those two fruits? Ain't I right, Brad?"

"You're right, Dad." Brad's smug expression made her want to remove the look right off his face.

"You need some sense knocked into you. To come back where you belong." Her father balled up a meaty fist as if he was the one to do it.

"Dear, why don't you come in the kitchen?" Her mother babbled, clucking around like a hen. She took two steps toward Dinah, eyes on her husband. She stopped, looking at him timidly. Her father hadn't given her permission to come closer.

"No, Mom." She looked her father in the face. "I'm not a whore. I don't like you calling me one every time I do something you don't agree with."

"Who do you think you're talking to, missy?" Her father struggled to his feet, glowering at her with storms in his gray eyes.

"You."

Her father looked as if he was waiting for her to cower. She didn't. Instead, she met his eyes head on.

"Brad hit me. And I'm not going to take that. Nor will I take your name-calling anymore." She took a deep, cleansing breath. She didn't have to take this. She'd learned from her counselor how important it was to separate herself from things that made her feel weak. "Mom, I'm sorry, but until he gets his act together, I'm not going to be visiting."

"You'd stay away from your own kin? 'Cause of them fairies?"

"No, Dad. I'm not living with Ian and Taylor anymore. But even if I was, it's not because of them. It's because of me."

Dropping a kiss on her mother's cheek, she strode to the door and out of it.

She'd finally stood up to the one man she'd never thought she would. And a lightness sprung into her step.

* * *

The next morning, Dinah sighed, sitting at the wooden desk at her still so new job. She'd moved up as a personal secretary to an executive, a job she'd gone after voraciously. It had lots more responsibility, a real office not a cubicle, and more important, tasks to get done. And so far her reviews had been stellar. She could do this job.

After leaving her parents' home, she'd celebrated her victory. Alone, it all felt hollow. She shoved a pencil into the sharpener. There had been no one to share it with. Not only did she miss the guys' presence, she missed their friendship.

She'd wanted to prove she could stand on her own. Had she done that? She'd stood up to her father of all people. If that didn't prove what she could do, she didn't know what could. And their protectiveness of her had been that, true protection, not tearing her down like Brad and her Dad. Her counselor had pointed that out.

She swished her hair back.

How did she feel about being with them? Both of them. Her thoughts had often turned to her time with them during these past eight months. And after a while, it had ceased to elicit shame, instead, bringing forth passion. And love. She loved them both, always had. And maybe it was time to give into it, into her deepest desire.

Had they found someone new? Only one way to find out.

Dialing Ian's phone, she tapped her foot nervously under her desk. Taylor sometimes turned his cell phone off when he was on a job or she would try him, too.

"Ian here." His voice came across the line subdued, but sounding so wonderful.

"Hi, Ian, it's Dinah."

He sounded pleased. "Hi, Dinah. How are you?"

"I'm good." She paused. "I don't have a lot of time, but I wondered if you and Taylor were available tonight for dinner. My place." It was the first time they would be over to see it. Maybe they'd be feeding her by the time it was all over.

She could almost hear the eyebrow cock in Ian's voice. "You want us to come over for dinner?"

"Uh-huh. I do. I'd love it if you both would come…" She stopped, then quickly caught herself. "…over."

He choked back a laugh. "Nice catch. And I'll have to check with Taylor. But I think we'd love to come to dinner tonight."

"Call me back if it's a problem? Otherwise, I'll see you around sevenish?" She rubbed her other sweaty hand across her leg. Her heart pounded in her chest. She couldn't wait to see them, and intended to hang up before something negative came out like they'd found someone else.

"Unless you hear back from me, we'll be there. Dinah?"

"Yes, Ian."

"I've missed you." His low whisper had her senses humming.

A smile tugged at the corners of her mouth as warmth infused her belly. She traced the phone cord with one finger, wishing it were the man on the other end. "I've missed you, too. You and Taylor. See you both tonight."

Hanging up, she leaned back in her chair. The time slowed down to an elephant's crawl. She kept checking her watch, willing it to move faster.

"Dinah, I need you to take this report down to Jim Hasker."

"Sure." She got up from her chair, moving around her desk.

"Why don't you leave a few minutes early?" Mr. Rogels peered at her, as he handed her the manila folder full of papers. "You've put in some long hours lately."

"Thank you. I think I will." Grabbing her purse and the folder, she headed down for Hasker's office. She whistled, her steps light on the commercial carpet. Early was good – she'd get a shower before seeing her guys. Her steps quickened as her trek took her through where she'd once worked. She couldn't wait to get out of here. It'd be one step closer to home.

"Dinah!" Karen called to her, waving like mad from her cubicle.

"Hey, Karen." Slipping in the cubicle doorway, she approached Karen's cluttered desk, stopping for a minute.

"How have you been? I haven't seen you since you went upward."

"Been doing O.K." Clenching Karen's desk in her hands, she leaned into it. "I've been busy." Little ashes of guilt pinged her. She hadn't made a lot of effort to keep in touch. Karen was nice enough, but there was an oddness about her.

"I'm sure. You still separated from the hunks?"

"Mostly." She couldn't fight the smile that popped open her lips. Maybe not after tonight.

"Oh, tell me you aren't going back to that even as friends. I thought you were done with them." Karen's eyes narrowed, and her lips pursed as if she'd eaten an overripe persimmon.

Dinah's eyelids shuttered to almost closed. Karen had always joked about her being with Ian and Taylor sexually. What had made the sudden turnaround? "I never said I was done. I was on a break. In fact, I plan to be more than friends with them."

"You are a greedy little thing." The hostility in Karen's voice gave her pause.

Dinah shrugged, her shoulders going up and down. "I better get this report in."

"Yeah, you'd better."

Dinah turned to go but heard the muffled word tossed in her direction. "Slut."

She whipped around to confront Karen. "What did you call me?"

Karen's cheeks pinkened and her eyes flared with open dislike. "Slut. I thought after all that happened, you'd give up. Little mousy thing like you. I still can't believe you got that position upstairs. Who'd you sleep with?"

Dinah's heart pounded, knowledge running around her veins. "You did my car." An outlandish claim that she wasn't sure of, but somehow in the wacky scheme of things made sense.

Karen's smile sent a shudder along Dinah's spine. "Considering you were always so scared of being a whore, I figured that would put you in your place. Cockroach, too. And the stupid movie. You'd told me how much you hated it. I only regret I didn't get to see your reaction with that. Poor little scared Dinah. Makes me wanna barf."

"You bitch." Things that had left her troubled during her time with Ian and Taylor hadn't been random events at all. They'd been calculated movements to keep her off balance. She'd told Karen some of these things about herself when they'd been friends. How Karen had switched the movies, Dinah didn't know, but she wasn't about to ask. Karen had used her own revelations to upset her. Dammit.

"I'm no bitch. You're the whore. Taking on two men when some of us don't have any! You're like my sister. You reminded me of her from the very first."

"You are one troubled woman." Karen's sister had taken her husband a few years back. She'd always talked about her with such vehemence.

"No more so than you. Tell me, do they give it to you up your ass? How's that feel? A new asshole for the asshole."

A cleared throat took their attention off of each other. Karen's supervisor, Dinah's former boss, stood staring wide-eyed at them from the doorway to the cubicle. How long had she been standing there?

"Ms. Smith." Dinah's voice was as sharp as glass. She'd been seriously close to smacking Karen to next Sunday. But that would give the little witch too much satisfaction. Better to walk away with her job intact. And her guys.

"Hello, Dinah. How are things?"

"Good." She glared at Karen. "I better go before I say some things I'll regret."

"Don't worry about it, Dinah. I'll take care of the problem." Smith regarded Karen with a distasteful look. "You've gone too far this time. Vandalism is a crime."

"You should be punishing her. All sluts deserve what they get." Karen poked out her lip petulantly. "I'm on probation again, I guess."

"We'll discuss it in my office after you clean out your desk."

Karen let out a gasp as Dinah walked away.

* * *

Dinah tugged on the short denim skirt she'd changed into after her shower. It wasn't coming down any further. Shouldn't bother her, except she was nervous.

Maybe I should change.

No, this third attempt at an outfit was the one. It showed off her legs. She'd set the table in the good dishes, not china, but not plastic.

What if they had found...? No, she wasn't going to think about it.

The doorbell chimed at three after seven. Taking a deep breath, Dinah opened the door. Heaven stood waiting for her on the front steps.

Both had dressed in polo shirts and khakis. Ian held a plant with purple flowers, and Taylor toted a bottle of wine.

Her eyes feasted on them until Taylor cleared his throat. "Gonna let us in, darling?"

"Oh. Yeah. I am." She stepped aside, and they walked into the apartment they hadn't seen since delivering her furniture and boxes.

"Nice." Taylor scanned. Her living room was a little spartan, a couch, small TV on a cheap stand, and a chair. He held out the wine bottle. "We weren't sure what was on the menu, so we went with red wine."

She took it. "Thank you. You didn't have to do that. And it's baked parmesan chicken, green beans and corn."

"Yum. My favorites." Taylor watched her carefully.

"Mine, too." Ian held up the plant. "Where do you want this? It's lavender."

Her favorite scent. It shouldn't have made her eyes tear up. But they knew her so well. "The kitchen will be fine." She went through the opening to the kitchen, the two of them trailing behind her.

Ian set the plant on the kitchen table. After she'd set the wine down on the small counter that separated the kitchen and living room, she looked at them taking over her small kitchen with their presence. They both were so beautiful. So edible. Emotion closed down her throat for a few moments before she could speak.

And they all started at the same time.

Ian laughed, his booming cadence more than filling up the rest of the small space. "Ladies first."

Taylor nodded, leaning back on booted heels.

"Dinner will be ready in about five minutes." She absently checked the timer as she muttered softly, "Are you two seeing anyone else?" Best to get that out of the way first.

"Huh?" Ian wore a puzzled expression.

But Taylor's eyes gleamed. "Yeah, what did you say?" His whole demeanor showed he'd heard her.

"You heard me." She licked her lips. Taylor's eyes followed the motion, his body tensing.

"I didn't." Ian's bounced his gaze between them.

"Because you're old, old man." Ian was about a year older than Taylor and her. Ribbing him about that was a Taylor pastime.

"Shaddup. What did you say, Di?"

Tracing her toe along a seam in the golden vinyl, she repeated, "Are you seeing anyone else these days?"

"Oh." Ian scratched his chin thoughtfully. "Are we? I'm sometimes so old I forget things."

She playfully smacked at his arm. And the next thing she knew, she was surrounded by two hard male bodies who smelled of spices and cedar.

"How could we? When we missed you." Taylor rubbed his chin on the top of her head, nuzzling.

She blew out a deep throated sigh. They hadn't found anyone else. Maybe she still had a shot to claim what she should have long before.

"Is that a good thing?" Ian stroked a hand along her shoulder.

"A very good thing." Leaning into their bodies was like coming home after a horrid day to a nice warm bed. The thrills and chills raced through her. Maybe make that a warm bed with a vibrator. Yeah, that was more like them. Safety, comfort and multiple orgasms. "I love you." She directed it to them both. "And I'm ready."

"Ready to..." Taylor trailed off, his words a rumble under her ear. He lifted her head by placing a finger under her chin. "I want to be sure, Di. No misunderstandings."

"I'm ready to be in a relationship with you both. If you still want me." There. She'd said it.

Taylor's breath whistled in his chest. And then, he and Ian hi-fived over her head.

"Thank god. We have missed you so much." Taylor pulled her out of Ian's arms and swung her around.

She giggled as her legs tapered out. "You goof. Put me down."

"Please say you're moving back in with us." Ian leaned back against the wall, a grin plotted firmly on his relaxed face. His trousers had tented up, showing how happy he was about the situation.

Taylor set her down on her feet, and kissed her wildly before she could answer. His hands were suddenly everywhere, rubbing her back, one hand palming a breast. He rubbed his cock against her, the hardness pressing into her like an arrow.

The timer rang.

Dinah pulled back, trying to extricate herself from Taylor's firm grasp.

He wouldn't let her go. "Let it burn," he murmured against her lips, his hands still roaming.

Ian snickered. "I don't think he's going to release you right now. Why don't you tell me what to do?"

Like she could with Taylor's mouth and hands on her. Unable to think, she leaned back slightly. "Taylor, let me get dinner out." Even as much as she wanted this with them, she wanted it to be perfect.

With a growl, he released her. "Hurry it up then, darling."

Shivering at the want and need reflected in his voice, she grabbed pot holders and dashed to the oven, pulling out the chicken. She cursed a couple of dark places. The guys would have to live with them for not letting her get it out right away. Pulling the corn coblets' pan off the hot burner, she then pulled the green bean casserole from the oven, too.

Taking the chicken pan in an oven-mitted hand, she said, "Why don't you two have a seat? Plates are out."

"You're killing me, darling." Taylor let out a long sigh. She heard footsteps on the linoleum.

"Hey! At least you got a make out. I haven't even gotten a kiss." Ian sounded pouty as she heard chairs scrape across the floor.

"You'll get yours later, I promise." Now this was what she had missed.

Chapter Nine

Dinah brought over the pan of chicken.

Taylor stood up right as she reached the table, pushing aside his chair.

"Where are you going? I have this under control."

"There's no silverware here, Di." He motioned with a hand, indicating the table, taking a step away.

"I know."

Taylor stopped mid-step, frozen in confusion.

Ian searched her face with dawning understanding. His voice was soft and husky as he spoke. "Taylor, you remember our first night as a couple?"

"Oh, yeah." Taylor's eyes glazed over with that thought.

"I had told Dinah when she came into our relationship, I'd be feeding her in Scottish tradition. I think she's turning the tables on me."

Taylor slowly sat back down.

"You're right. I have one change to that tradition." She walked back to get the rest of the food.

"What's that?" Ian leaned back in his chair.

"I want to feed you both since I'm coming into your relationship. That's why I'm the only one with a fork."

"You're going to feed us from across the table?" Taylor looked dubiously at the plate set up.

Well, that wasn't going to work, even across her small table. Her arms weren't that long. So much for her bright idea. "Oh, no."

Immediately, Ian got up, pushing his chair closer to Taylor's. He got another chair and set it on the same side of the table as them. "How's that? You can be in the middle."

She shivered, Goosebumps erupted on her chilled skin. "Nice place to be." Even better for after dinner. She settled in the chair beside Taylor as Ian plopped down next to her.

Taylor leaned down to kiss her head. "Wait until later. You're going to find out how nice."

"I hope I do." She rubbed one hand along her thigh. The whole thing of coming into their relationship did scare her just a little bit. Being part of a permanent relationship with two others was something she'd never done before.

"You will." Ian dropped his hand to rub along her bared leg. "I like this skirt. But not as much as I'm going to enjoy taking it off of you."

Swallowing, she looked forward to see Taylor putting a big piece of chicken on her plate. "Hey. I'm supposed to serve."

"Hey yourself. You'll feed me. But let's get this show on the road."

"Geesh. You'd think you hadn't had sex in weeks." She slowly cut up the chicken even as he dumped vegetables on her plate.

Ian's shoulders shook with laughter. "He is a horny thing. We haven't been with a woman since you. I think he's missed it."

"No. I've missed Dinah."

Closing her eyes, she sat for a moment. She'd never expected the onslaught of emotion doing this. They'd never be able to all three marry or have any kind of formal commitment. No one would understand their relationship outside of a few with that lifestyle. But it was the most loving, stable thing she'd ever be involved in.

Her lids opening, she picked up chicken on her fork. "Here you go." First bite was offered to Taylor. Next one went to Ian. His mouth closed slowly around it, looking in her eyes the whole time. Slowly, she fed them and herself dinner.

"I'm thirsty." Taylor nodded with his head to the empty wine goblet in front of her.

Crap. She'd forgotten that.

Ian rose to his feet, sauntering to the wine bottle. "I'll get it. One glass? I guess you're taking care of that, too?"

"I sure am."

He found an opener and deftly got out the cork. He poured the glass about half full with hands that trembled slightly.

So she wasn't the only one a little nervous.

Holding up the small corn coblet smeared with butter, she offered it to Ian. He nibbled, then moved to her fingers on the ends, circling one with his tongue. "Hey, eat the corn. Not me."

"Honey, I don't think you'll be saying that later." He cocked his head to the side. "Hmm. Butter on your lips." His head ducked in to savor her mouth. "Damn, didn't get it." He went in again and again.

"Yeah, buddy, I think her mouth is clean." Taylor folded his arms across his chest in mock irritation.

"Yours isn't." Ian leaned in and so did Taylor, and they kissed forcefully in front of her.

Oh, my.

Something about the two men kissing stirred something within her. Heat roared to the surface in her ears and cheeks.

In unison, as if they knew of the desire sweeping her, Taylor's lips left Ian's to plunder hers, while Ian attacked her neck. Someone's hands settled on her chest while another hand slid across her inner thigh to touch and stroke her through her panties.

"Guys. We aren't done..." Her breath huffed in her chest. Not that this should stop. Ever.

"Yeah, we are." Taylor inhaled against her mouth, his warm breath mingling with hers.

Ian's nod was felt along her neck, tickling it. "Oh, yeah. You fed us plenty."

Oh, god, what those nimble fingers and mouths did to her even while she was completely clothed. "Bedroom?"

Taylor groaned, his lips hardly pulling away from hers. "I don't want to let you go." His hand clutched tightly at her shoulders.

"C'mon, lover." Ian withdrew from them, standing up. His visible erection strained against the material of his pants. "We'll be more comfortable."

Taylor tossed her up in his arms, his lips continuing to probe hers until he almost ran her head into a wall because he wasn't looking where he was going. "Dammit."

"Let's not hurt the woman." Ian followed along behind them. "You need to slow down, man."

"I know. I know." Taylor sounded breathless. The haste that he showed about wanting her sent heat flaring down to her belly. She'd never been desired this badly.

"That door there." She pointed to her bedroom, the master in her small apartment.

Into the room Taylor darted, pushing open the door almost into the wall. Ian switched on the lamp on her nightstand. She'd cleaned up after she'd gotten home, making the bed and putting everything away.

Taylor carefully lowered her on top of the blue and white flowered coverlet. A sachet of cinnamon rested on the night table, filling the air with its scent. That was why she'd shut the door, to trap it inside. She'd been trying to make her room as nice as possible for tonight.

Taylor pulled his shirt over his head, dropping it on the floor.

Her eyes surveyed the space taken up by Ian and her already. Their bed was huge. Hers was a full – plenty for her, but for three people…"I hadn't even thought about how small my bed is." Maybe this wasn't a good idea? Her hands tightened by her side. No, she wanted this. Tonight and every night after.

Taylor smiled and unbuttoned his pants. "You're moving in with us, aren't you? Our bed is plenty big."

"I am. If you want me to."

Taylor shook his head. "Of course, we do, darling."

Ian clucked his tongue. "Yeah, we'll have to sleep on top of each other tonight. I might have to sleep inside of you. You know, to make more room." He winked at her.

Her thighs clenched together. Now that was the way to get no sleep at all.

"One more question." Taylor paused a moment. "Lube and condoms? Please tell me you have some."

"My nightstand drawer." She wiggled over the bed to retrieve them, laying them in a more accessible spot. Her cheeks warmed at Ian's knowing grin. She'd gotten them a while back, not knowing if she'd ever get to use them.

"Aren't you 'Little Miss Prepared'?"

"She always was." Taylor shimmied down his pants.

She moaned at the exposed skin he displayed. He shook his butt, probably knowing they were both looking. Nibbling on those washboard abs, that perfect cock, those rounded globes. His well-defined muscles looked even bigger than she remembered.

"Have you been working out more?" she blurted it out, then cringed.

Taylor nodded, stepping out of the pants.

"You're in a hurry." Ian leaned back as Taylor stalked toward him. Taylor dove in for a kiss, his hand going between Ian's legs to grasp him through his pants.

Dinah watched, her sex becoming even slicker with moisture.

Taylor's hand found hers, and he guided her to Ian's cock, pressing her hand down to grasp it. Slowly, she began to rub and squeeze as Taylor did the same while he kissed Ian hard and deep.

Ian came up for air. "Guess you are in a hurry." He shrugged off his shirt in one fluid motion.

Taylor's hand left hers to grasp his zipper, pulling it down. Dinah pulled her hand away. After Ian's pants came down, she placed her hand back on the smooth surface of Ian's hard cock. Such velvety bigness.

She continued to stroke Ian as Taylor kissed down his chest. She let go as he kissed over the planes of Ian's belly until he reached his cock. His fingers stroked around the tip, dipping into the pre-come that had leaked since they'd been touching him.

Her eyes drifted to Taylor's own neglected cock. It rested, flushed and hard against Taylor's body, which was stretched out in a curve to Ian's feet. No sense in it being lonely since she had a free mouth.

"Can I...?" She took a breath and licked her lips. *Be bold.* "Can I touch you?"

Taylor wiggled his hips around to where she had a good angle of access. "Darling, you don't have to ask. Ever."

Her hand grasped his smooth thickness, sliding him up and down. His hips arched. A wicked thought came, and she stopped. His breathing evened out as he cupped Ian with his own hands.

Grabbing the cherry-flavored lube, she spread some on her hands and warmed it. The sweet smell filled the room over the cinnamon. She slowly slid both hands around Taylor on either side. Her hands were so slick he slipped right into them. She moved them up and down, the slippery friction delighting her.

He hissed, his hands gripping the sheet, having dropped away from Ian.

Ian's soft laughter echoed as he sat up a little more beside Taylor, taking a look. "Hard to concentrate, lover?"

"I'll give you hard to concentrate." A growl rolled up in Taylor's chest. He pushed Ian's hips down with his hands, sliding himself down, too, and sucked Ian's cock into his mouth.

Ian's hips bucked. Dinah watched, captivated, then with a wiggle of Taylor's cock, remembered where her hands rested. Playfully, she captured him tightly in her hands, cupping him and moving up and down quickly with her hands surrounding him like a channel.

He moaned. His hips rocked in time with her hands.

She lowered her head. Opening her mouth, she sucked his tip in, her hands still clutching him. Cherry dripped onto her willing tongue along with a taste of something wholly Taylor. She opened wide to pull his swollen cock as far as she could get it into her mouth, one hand steadying the base.

She bobbled her mouth up and down around him, concentrating on the feast in front of her. His hips bucked more wildly with each surrounding of her mouth.

Dinah pulled away from Taylor as he broke off what he was doing to Ian with a popping sound.

Taylor panted, his body shivering with arousal. She wiped her mouth, which was wet with cherry lube. His cock glistened in the low lamplight.

"Dammit." Ian took a deep breath, sinking down into the sheets.

Dinah looked from Taylor to Ian. What came now?

Taylor smiled, leaning in for a quick kiss on her lips. He cocked his head to the side, looking down her body. "Too many clothes on. Didn't we have that problem last time?"

Ian tugged on the bottom of her sweater, lifting it. "We did." He pulled it over her head. Unsnapping her bra, he replaced the silky material with his hands. "God, you're beautiful." His hands slid like satin across her skin. His hands were always so smooth.

Taylor tugged on her legs. "Lift up. Much as I like the skirt, it needs to come off." Sliding the skirt down as Ian stopped a moment to help, Taylor tugged off her underwear at the same time. He tossed them on the floor. "Very wet, darling."

Her cheeks heated in embarrassment as Ian's hands found a particularly sensitive part of her nipples. No, she wouldn't be embarrassed. They knew her passion for them. And there was nothing wrong with that. Why had she fought this for so long?

"I love you." She licked her lips, nervousness mixing in with arousal. "But how...do I fit into all this?"

Taylor groaned. "Darling, you'll fit just fine."

Ian took a deep breath, collecting himself, stretching back his shoulders. "I'm going to take you from the front. Taylor's going to take you from behind." He looked at Taylor with a serious expression. "She's nervous, man."

Taylor pulled her into a hug, his hands stroking her hair. "There's nothing to be nervous about."

"I've never...never..."

He kissed the top of her head. "We know, darling."

Ian nodded, pointing to the lube. "We'll use plenty of that. We'd never hurt you."

She looked into both of their loving faces. "I know. I trust you."

Ian tugged her off of Taylor's lap to lay her down on her side in the middle of the bed. He ran a finger from her breastbone to her belly button. "So lovely." He leaned in to kiss her and slowly worked his way down, nipping at her collarbone.

Taylor's hands massaged her back, kneading with all his precision. His hands rasped against the skin, having been roughened from all his woodworking.

Ian rested his head eye level with her breasts. He sucked a nipple part of the way into his mouth, suckling it. Her back arched, but Taylor continued to pleasure her.

When Taylor reached her butt, he massaged both ass cheeks. Swallowing, she tensed to see what he was planning. But then, Ian reached her stomach, planting wide kisses along the bottom of it. Her breath hitched at what he was looking to do next.

Ian looked up at her, his eyes half lidded. "Now for dessert." His long tongue parted her, licking her up and down before suckling her into his mouth completely.

She moaned, the sensations overwhelming. Her entire body energized, nerve endings budding to the surface.

Ian's wide ranging tongue found every sensitive spot she had. She soon writhed under his touch.

A single slippery finger breached her bottom. She couldn't stiffen. Not with what was being done in the front.

Cool liquid flowed down around her anus. More of the sweet scent filled the air.

More pressure. Taylor had added a finger.

Ian circled her clit with his tongue, sliding a finger into her channel with an in and out motion so like what he'd be doing soon with his cock. So good, it shook away all her nervousness. All she could do was feel.

Taylor added a third finger as the orgasm swelled and burst inside of her. Her body spasmed, and her breath caught in her chest.

Using fingers and mouths, they brought her over the brink twice more. She'd never been wetter. And the fingers had ceased to hurt her; she wasn't even sure how many there were.

Slowly drifting back to herself from her third orgasm, she stiffened as more pressure came along her bottom. She heard a squeezing sound as more lube was added to the fingers pleasuring her there.

"Shhhh." Taylor's guttural voice came from against her back, as his other hand massaged the small of it with gentle circular motions.

Ian planted one last kiss on her clitoris. After sheathing on a condom, he kissed lazily up her body until he reached her mouth. As his tongue breached her lips, so did his cock slide into her, going all the way in, grinding down inside of her.

Her body arched again, tightening around Taylor's fingers.

Taylor chuckled softly. "I will need my fingers back eventually." As she relaxed her muscles, he withdrew his fingers.

Ian thrust into her, setting up a rhythm, making her burn again.

Her heart pounded. Taylor pushed her more onto Ian, impaling him deeper within her sex. Ian groaned, grasping her hips and keeping the deep penetration.

Taylor spread her cheeks with his hands, wiggling his cock against her bottom. Was this going to hurt?

A little at a time, Taylor pushed into her. Slowly, he took his time penetrating her, taking each little centimeter he could, then easing back. Ian worked with him, moving in synch.

The pressure was intense with this double penetration. But as each stroke sparked along her senses, she rocked alongside them, helpless in a web they'd created around her.

When he was almost fully in, Taylor's breathing hitched. His voice came roughly as he nipped her neck. "Am I hurting you?"

She warmed at his question. Even now he loved her enough to ask. There was a lot of pressure, a lot of stretching. But he'd taken it slowly, there hadn't been too much hurting. It was hard to tell where pain began and pleasure stopped. And nothing had ever been this intimate. "No."

"Good."

She had two guys within her. Her guys. She was fully theirs. They'd claimed her.

As if they'd heard her thought, they both said, "Mine," at the same time.

The words drove her over the precipice into her orgasm. She screamed, words unintelligible, unable to get close enough to either of them as they pounded into her.

Taylor's whole body stiffened as his hips flattened against her as much as possible. His cock pumped within her, his orgasm holding him in its grip.

Ian's shout came next, as he called her name, his body spasming in his release.

They lay there in the still of the room after everyone's climax stopped, Taylor behind her, no longer inside her. Ian rested in front of her, his spent cock still lying within her depths.

Ian slowly pulled out of her, her moisture gushing out with his withdrawal. "I can't move."

Taylor's muffled voice spoke. "You just did."

"Oh. Yeah." Ian stripped off the condom, yanking off Taylor's, too. "Are you all right, honey?" He tossed them in the trash and rejoined them in the small bed. "We didn't hurt you, did we?"

"I'm...wonderful." She was. Her body had a delicious tiredness to it. As Taylor wrapped his arms around her, snuggling into her back and as Ian wrapped himself cozily around her front, she closed her eyes.

She'd given into her darkest desire. And found her home.

DINAH'S CHRISTMAS DESIRE

Wearing underwear and a bra, Dinah fingered the velvety material of the dress lying on the bed. The softness slipped across her fingers.

She heard the footsteps a second before hands touched her back. "Need help with the zipper, darling?" Taylor murmured as he came up behind her.

"I don't have on the dress, silly." Her breathing increased, along with her heart rate. She didn't turn to face him but leaned back into his muscular, shirtless body.

"Guess I can't help with that yet." Fingers caressed along her ribs. Her nerve endings jingled as he reached around to her middle. He slid his hands down over her bare stomach and then across her underwear. He moved his fingers quickly back and forth just over her clit, teasing her through the material. "I can help with other things." One finger pressed in on the nub.

"This is helping?" She sucked in a shaky breath. Her body went slack, leaning against him.

"That's more than helping her with her zipper." Ian's amused voice sounded from behind them.

"Maybe you could do better?" Taylor nipped her shoulder as his fingers continued to toy through the thin cloth of her panties. Dinah shuddered. Her arousal seeped out as all the things they could do this evening came to mind.

Ian came alongside of them, carrying two small packages. "Merry Christmas." He handed a green one toward Taylor and a red one to Dinah.

Taylor dropped his hands from Dinah's mid-section and turned to face Ian. Her sex protested their absence. Taylor accepted his present.

"What's this?" Dinah held the small parcel in her hands as she turned to face Ian, too.

Ian had already dressed for the evening. She sighed. They would never convince him not to go to this Christmas Eve party. But she'd rather stay home and make some magic between the three of them under the mistletoe. So, tradition spoke only of kissing under it. Didn't mean it had to stop there.

With a mischievous grin, Ian said, "Open it." He sat on the bed with legs spread open. The bulge of his cock was outlined by his thin black pants. "Not me, Dinah. It." Once upon a time, being caught staring would have made her shy. Now, it only made her smile. He waved a hand. "Go ahead."

Taylor tore into the wrapping. "Oh, it's been a long time, man." His mouth quirked up into a grin. "Too long." She glanced over to read from the package. He'd opened a vibrating anal plug.

She blinked. It had a remote. "A butt plug?"

"Oh, yeah." Taylor ripped into it before taking the device out to hand to Ian. "You doing the honors?"

"After Dinah opens hers."

"It's not Christmas yet. Or are you trying to be naughty?" She looked warily at the gift.

"I'm always naughty. I want you and Taylor to have these presents early. We always opened one the night before Christmas. I'm just choosing which ones you two open tonight."

Taylor swiftly unbuttoned the top to his pants before dropping them to the floor. His cock sprang up, huge in front of his body.

Dinah couldn't tear her eyes away as he got on the bed. He shifted up on hands and knees, butt in the air. Then, he wiggled his naked self back and forth, knowing that they watched.

"Open it, Dinah." Ian tilted his head to the side as he watched Taylor, unable to look away as well.

She quickly tore off the paper. Looked down to find a vibrating egg with a remote. Pulling her gaze up from it, she watched as Ian got on the bed behind Taylor. "Are we wearing these to the party?" Her heart raced. This wasn't anything she'd done before. A vibrator? In public? Her mouth dried with her excitement. "Won't people hear them?"

Ian squirted some lube into his hands, warming it up. "I doubt anyone's heard the anal plug. The vibrator is supposed to be quiet. And it'll be tucked up inside of you."

Her whole body rocked to its core. Now, what he'd said primed her desire, but it wasn't as stimulating as the scene in front of her. Taylor's head came up as Ian penetrated him with the plug.

Not a more perfect sight had ever been seen, except maybe when Ian was naked, too. Two muscular men draped all over each other. *Her men.* She bit her lip. The two of them making out could be almost as sexy as it was with her in the middle…but only almost.

"It's in." One of Ian's hands went around to cup Taylor's cock, cresting around it. The other took a small black key ring from his pocket. Pushing a button, Ian cocked his head as Taylor's body straightened out in a line. "It works."

Taylor's hips bucked. "No shit."

Her breathing erratic, Dinah slipped on the bed behind Ian. "Why are we going out tonight?"

"He wants to torture us." Taylor's voice came muffled. "Can we get on with the party, so we can hurry home?"

Ian clicked off the remote before slipping it in his pocket. His hand withdrew from Taylor as Dinah plastered herself against Ian's back. She rubbed her breasts against him. Her hands skimmed to his hips.

"I want to try these out. We don't have to stay long." Ian extricated himself, taking the vibrator from Dinah's hands. "Take off your underwear. I'll help you put it in."

"Five minutes?" Taylor turned over to rock to his feet, moving out of the way. "Lay back, darling."

"More than five. I have two remotes to hit."

Dinah eased off the bikini briefs she wore. She reclined back on the pillows in the spot that Taylor had vacated. Spreading her thighs, she licked her lips.

Taylor rewarded her with a groan while Ian swallowed audibly. Both sets of eyes remained on her wide open sex.

"Stay home?" She pulled her bottom lip up between her teeth. "You could still torture us. We could have dinner here."

"Wait a minute. Two remotes?" Taylor arched a brow. "If you take mine, why don't I get hers?"

"Because that's not the way it works." Ian opened the package. The egg slid out into his fingers. He wiped it off and held it in his hands. "Don't want it to be cold." He kneeled on the bed in front of Dinah.

"Bastard." Taylor swatted Ian's backside.

"Cut that out. And you'll be doing me by the deer in the front yard by the time we make it home. Mark my words."

Taylor didn't deny it.

Dinah opened her legs wider as Ian pressed the small cylinder up into her center. Her juices coated his hand. He bent his head, nostrils flaring. His fingers brushed her clit, and as though he couldn't resist, he twiddled with the bundle of nerves. She thrust herself against him.

Taylor cleared his throat. Ian quickly pulled away. He licked his fingers one by one. "You're going to be so wet later." He took her underwear in a shaking hand. Sliding it over a foot, he said, "Get her dress, Taylor." He slipped the underwear back into place.

Taylor held out the dress as Ian helped her up. Together, they slid it on and zipped it.

Ian blew out a low whistle. "Santa baby is right."

The short dress, which resembled a Santa suit, tightly hugged her curves. She smoothed it down. "Like?"

Taylor pressed a kiss to the side of her neck. "Oh, yeah."

He quickly dressed while she put on hose and then followed her downstairs.

In the living room, sparkling lights beamed their brilliant hues from the Christmas tree. Three red stockings, each with one of their names written in silver glitter, hung from the mantel. Each time she saw them, warmth spread through her. Who'd have thought she could be so happy with her two guys on their first Christmas together? Certainly not her until they'd shown her how life could be in a threesome.

She walked to the tree, hugging herself around her middle.

"Everything all right?" Taylor came up behind her to place his arms around her.

"Everything's perfect." She let out a contented sigh.

"Where's Ian?" He nuzzled her neck.

"I don't know, but he's taking too long."

Ian stomped in the front door. White powder clung to his hair and clothes. "It's snowing. I had to go see for myself."

"Really?" Dinah stepped to the window to peer outside. White flakes twirled as they fell to the ground. Even more perfect. They'd have a white Christmas to commemorate their first holiday together.

Taylor leaned into her body as he peeked. "Sure is." His masculine scent overtook the pine Christmas tree smell. She nuzzled against his neck.

A buzz startled her. Her pelvis tilted around the now vibrating egg. Spasms rocked her, which she couldn't control.

Taylor steadied her with his body.

Her world narrowed down to the pressure building and rocketing in her sex. And then, the vibrations increased.

She managed to look at Ian. The buzz ceased. "I forgot to test it upstairs. Guess it works?"

She growled. To hell with going out. She walked over to grasp his face in her hands. His eyes took on a glow of wonder as she stood on tiptoes to kiss him fully. Her tongue pressed against the seam of his mouth until he opened. She explored him much as if he were a candy cane hanging on their tree.

The buzzing began again. Her hips rocked into his. She whimpered against his lips.

One of his hands came up to press against a breast. The dress wouldn't allow him inside so he stroked outside the material, pinching and rolling the nipple between his fingers.

A body pressed against her back. Ian's mouth left hers to claim Taylor's as they kissed over her. Taylor's cock bumped up against her back while Ian's nudged her front. Ian's hands continued to caress her breasts while Taylor's rubbed the side of her hips.

She took a deep breath. "No party."

Ian's mouth barely left Taylor's. "Agreed."

Ha. She'd done it.

Taylor slowly edged them backward until they neared the tree. He pulled his mouth from Ian's and got a fleece blanket from the couch to spread on the floor before he lowered himself to it. "I'll make a fire later. But I need you two. Now." He let out a sudden, strangled moan.

Ian had activated the butt plug.

The vibrations increased in her sex as she went down to the blanket. Her torso rocked up beside Taylor's writhing form.

Ian knelt down beside them. "If I don't get to have my fun in public, I will have it here in private. This will be my present for tonight."

He reached out and pulled off Dinah's hose and underwear. She shifted, changing the angle of the vibrator. The orgasm hit her, a jumble of sensations running through her, quick and hard.

He wrestled the clothing from her feet before scooting to Taylor. "Feel good?" He reached his hand forward to fondle Taylor's cock. Taylor lifted up his hips to push more into Ian's hand.

"You know it does."

Ian's other hand went back into his pocket, and Taylor twisted upward again.

Dinah's own vibrations changed into a pulse pattern. *Ease off. Buzz. Ease off. Buzz.* She let out another sound. Her hands clenched into fists. Nothing had prepared her for this. Arousal built up from seeing Taylor and from the egg lodged inside of her. Her eyes squinted shut. The orgasm cut through her, leaving her moaning.

Her eyes opened to find that Ian had undone Taylor's pants and slipped them off. He stroked Taylor's cock, rolling his hand around it. Taylor thrust in time, more than likely to the anal plug.

Ian saw her watching. One hand left Taylor to reach into his pocket. The egg changed patterns yet again, now doing a long buzz and a short pause.

Her body rained down its juices. Her clit pulsed in time with the vibrator.

Again, it changed to a steady slow buzz.

A strangled cry from Taylor broke the quiet. She glanced over to see him pumping his cock into Ian's mouth as he orgasmed.

Taylor lay back, breathing like a freight train. The glittering tree lights reflected on his face. After a minute, he grabbed Ian, pulling him in for a fast and furious kiss.

Dinah reached down to pull out the vibrator.

They broke apart to stare at her.

She met Ian's gaze. "It's his turn, don't you think, Taylor?"

Taylor reached into Ian's pocket, taking both remotes. He switched the vibrators off. "Oh, yeah." He grinned. "Take mine out." Ian helped him take out the anal plug. Then Taylor shifted over behind Ian, pulling him to recline against him as Taylor rested his back on the wall beside the hearth.

She quickly turned her back to them. "Zipper."

Ian's hands shook as he pulled the tab down. She shrugged out of the dress as Ian blew out a breath. "My Christmas angel."

No, they'd been the angels to her. They'd shown her the way. She reached around to unclasp her bra before slipping it off.

She shimmied over to them on her knees. Sliding the tab to Ian's zipper down, she winked at Taylor. "Help me? Someone's been naughty."

His smile was huge. "You got it, darling."

Ian's voice came on a breath. "Don't you two double team me." He reached out to caress her breast.

She pulled back. "No. This is your turn." She nodded to Taylor, who grasped both of Ian's hands in his.

Taylor kissed the side of his neck. "Relax, Ian."

With a sigh, he did.

She slid Ian's pants down and shifted her body over him. She placed her sex directly over Ian's rigid cock. Her hand came down to help guide him slowly into her channel.

Ian hissed as he penetrated her sex.

She lifted up again until the tip of his cock was the only thing inside her. Then, she planted herself back down. Repeating the actions, she squeezed in with her walls, clenching around him on each downturn of her body.

Ian's hands whitened in Taylor's, but Taylor didn't release him.

She rolled herself back before grinding her pelvis as hard as she could against him, unable to get close enough. Ian's moan rumbled up deep from within him as he came, his hips thrusting forward wildly to fill her like she wanted.

After a moment, Taylor released Ian, who lay down in a daze with her cuddled beside him. Taylor grabbed a blanket to toss over them before lying down.

Ian kissed her cheek. "Merry Christmas, Dinah."

Taylor kissed the other side. "Merry Christmas, darling."

The tree lights twinkled. "Only because of you two." She let out a contented sigh. "I'm glad you two aren't like Christmas."

"Why's that?" Ian snuggled more into her.

"Because it only comes once a year."

Mechele Armstrong

Have you ever wondered, "What if crayons have a kingdom?" Mechele Armstrong did at age five. Now, turning the imagination of a wide-eyed child into intense spellbinding stories for adults, she is winning over new fans every day.

Writing stories and poetry as a hobby, she graduated from Virginia Commonwealth University with a degree in Religious Studies and Social Welfare. Although there were challenges with work and family, the need to write and be published, to share her passion for books, was always there.

During a rainy weekend at the beach reading several romance novels she fell in love, not with the hero, but with the genre again. So began a two-year adventure of doing what she loved most, creating worlds with strong heroines and enchanting heroes that will keep you turning pages until the end.

Using the Internet and the local Romance Writer's Association, she learned and refined her craft. Living in Virginia with a husband, kids, dog, and fish, she finds time to share her vivid imagination and ability to tell stories of adventure, love, lust, and everything in between.

Find out more about Mechele by visiting her website at http://www.mechelearmstrong.com, or send an email to her at mechele@mechelearmstrong.com.

Printed in the United States
128956LV00007B/2/A